I0734143

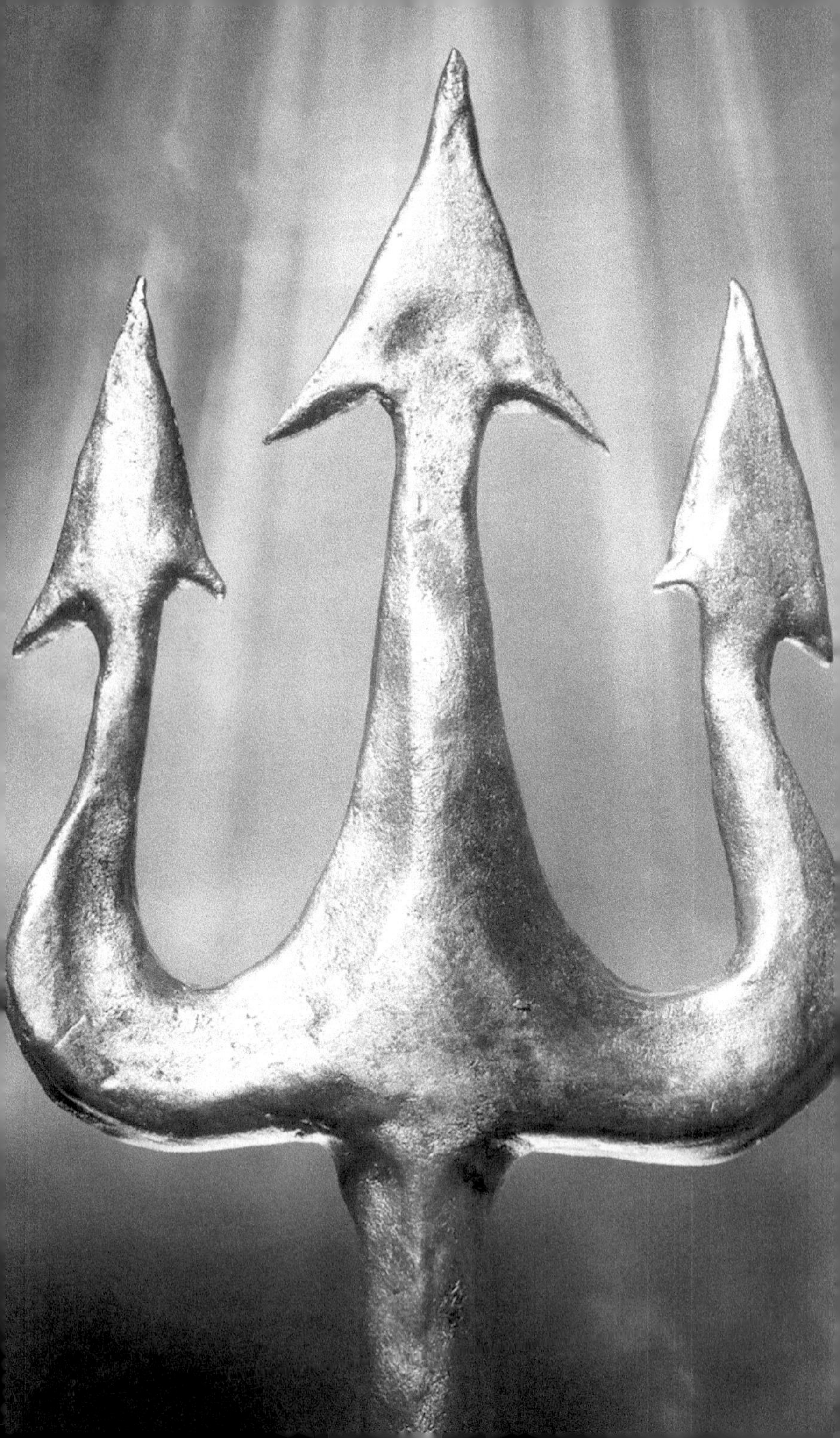

OPTION
Number Three

Trident Security Book 10

SAMANTHA COLE

OPTION NUMBER THREE

Copyright ©2017 Samantha A. Cole
All Rights Reserved.
Suspenseful Seduction Publishing
Option Number Three is a work of fiction. Names, characters, businesses, organizations, places, events, and incidents either are the product of the author's imagination or are used fictitiously. Any resemblance to actual persons, living or dead, events, or locales is entirely coincidental.

Cover by Samantha A. Cole
Photographer: Golden Czermak
Model: Michael Scanlon
Edited by Eve Arroyo - www.evearroyo.com

No part of this book may be reproduced, scanned or distributed in any printed or electronic form without permission. Please do not participate in or encourage piracy of copyrighted materials in violation of the author's rights. Purchase only authorized editions.

Okay, this might sound weird, but this book is dedicated to my fur babies, who constantly put up with me saying, "Give me one more minute, I mean, five more minutes to finish this scene, and then we'll go for a walk."

ACKNOWLEDGMENTS

I'd like to thank the following people:

My friends and family for all their support over the past two years.

My beta readers:
Allena, Brandie, Charla, Debbie, Felisha, Jen, Jessica, Joanne, Julie, Katie, and Milynn.

My editor, Eve.

My Sexy Six-Pack Sirens Facebook group for their shout outs, whip cracking, and everyday fun.

Last, but far from least, my readers. Without you, I would have never have come this far.

AUTHOR'S NOTE

The story within these pages is completely fictional but the concepts of BDSM are real. If you do choose to participate in the BDSM lifestyle, please research it carefully and take all precautions to protect yourself. Fiction is based on real life but real life is *not* based on fiction. Remember-Safe, Sane and Consensual!

***While not every character is in every book, these are the ones with the most mentions throughout the series. This guide will help keep readers straight about who's who.

Trident Security (TS) is a private investigative and military agency, co-owned by Ian and Devon Sawyer. With governmental and civilian contracts, the company got its start when the brothers and a few of their teammates from SEAL Team Four retired to the private sector. The original six-man team is referred to as the Sexy Six-Pack, as they were dubbed by Kristen Sawyer, née Anders, or the Alpha Team. Trident had since expanded and former members of the military and law enforcement have been added to the staff. The company is located on a guarded compound, which was a former import/export company cover for a drug trafficking operation in Tampa, Florida. Three warehouses on the property were converted into large apartments, the TS offices, gym, and bunk rooms. There is also an obstacle course, a Main Street shooting gallery, a helicopter pad, and more features necessary for training and missions.

In addition to the security business, there is a fourth warehouse that now houses an elite BDSM club, co-owned by Devon, Ian, and their cousin, Mitch Sawyer, who is the manager. A lot of time and money has gone into making The Covenant the most sought after membership in the Tampa/St. Petersburg area and beyond. Members are thoroughly vetted before being granted access to the elegant club.

There are currently over fifty Doms who have been appointed Dungeon Masters (DMs), and they rotate two or three shifts each throughout the month. At least four DMs are on duty at all times at various posts in the pit, playrooms, and the new garden, with an additional one roaming around. Their job is to ensure the safety of all the submissives in the club. They step in if a sub uses their safeword and the Dom in the scene doesn't hear or heed it, and make sure the equipment used in scenes isn't harming the subs.

The Covenant's security team takes care of everything else that isn't scene-related, and provides safety for all members and are essentially the bouncers. With the recent addition of the garden, and more private, themed rooms, the owners have expanded their self-imposed limit of 350 members. The fire marshal had approved them for 500 when the warehouse-turned-kink club first opened, but the cousins had intentionally kept that number down to maintain an elite status. Now with more room, they are increasing the membership to 500, still under the new maximum occupancy of 720.

Between Trident Security and The Covenant there's plenty of romance, suspense, and steamy encounters. Come meet the Sexy Six-Pack, their friends, family, and teammates.

The Sexy Six-Pack (Alpha Team) and Their Significant Others

- Ian "Boss-man" Sawyer: Devon and Nick's brother; retired Navy SEAL; co-owner of Trident Security and The Covenant; husband/Dom of Angelina (Angel).
- Devon "Devil Dog" Sawyer: Ian and Nick's brother; retired Navy SEAL; co-owner of Trident Security and The Covenant; husband/Dom of Kristen; father of John Devon "JD."
- Ben "Boomer" Michaelson: retired Navy SEAL; explosives and ordnance specialist; husband/Dom of Katerina; son of Rick and Eileen.
- Jake "Reverend" Donovan: retired Navy SEAL; temporarily assigned to run the West Coast team; sniper; fiancé/Dom of Nick;

brother of Mike; Whip Master at The Covenant.

- Brody "Egghead" Evans: retired Navy SEAL; computer specialist; fiancé/Dom of Fancy.
- Marco "Polo" DeAngelis: retired Navy SEAL; communications specialist and back up helicopter pilot; husband/Dom of Harper; father to Mara.
- Nick "Junior" Sawyer: Ian and Devon's brother; current Navy SEAL; fiancé/submissive of Jake.
- Kristen "Ninja-girl" Sawyer: author of romance/suspense novels; wife/submissive of Devon; mother of "JD."
- Angelina "Angie/Angel" Sawyer: graphic artist; wife/submissive of Ian.
- Katerina "Kat" Michaelson: dog trainer for law enforcement and private agencies; wife/submissive of Boomer.
- Millicent "Harper" DeAngelis: lawyer; wife/submissive of Marco; mother of Mara.
- Francine "Fancy" Maguire: baker; fiancée/submissive of Brody.

Extended Family, Friends, and Associates of the Sexy Six-Pack

- Mitch Sawyer: Cousin of Ian, Devon, and

Nick; co-owner/manager of The Covenant, Dom.

- T. Carter: US spy and assassin; works for covert agency Deimos; Dom/boyfriend of Jordyn.
- Jordyn Alvarez: US spy and assassin; member of covert agency Deimos; submissive of Carter.
- Tyler Ellis: Stockbroker; lifestyle switch—Dom to Tori.
- Tori Freyja: K9 trainer for veterans in need of assistance/service dogs; submissive to Tyler.
- Parker Christiansen: owner of New Horizons Construction; husband/Dom of Shelby; adoptive father of Franco and Victor.
- Shelby Christiansen: stay-at-home mom; two-time cancer survivor; wife/submissive of Parker; adoptive mother of Franco and Victor.
- Curt Bannerman: retired Navy SEAL; owner of Halo Customs, a motorcycle repair and detail shop; husband of Dana; stepfather of Ryan, Taylor, Justin, and Amanda. Lives in Iowa.
- Dana Prichard-Bannerman: teacher; widow of retired SEAL Eric Prichard; wife

of Curt; mother of Ryan, Taylor, Justin, and Amanda. Lives in Iowa.

- Jenn "Baby-girl" Mullins: college student; goddaughter of Ian; "niece" of Devon, Brody, Jake, Boomer, and Marco; father was a Navy SEAL; parents murdered.
- Mike Donovan: owner of the Irish pub, Donovan's; brother of Jake.
- Charlotte "Mistress China" Roth: Parole officer; Domme and Whip Master at The Covenant.
- Travis "Tiny" Daultry: former professional football player; head of security at The Covenant and Trident compound; occasional bodyguard for TS.
- Doug "Bullseye" Henderson: retired Marine; head of the Personal Protection Division of TS.
- Rick and Eileen Michaelson: Boomer's parents; guardians of Alyssa. Rick is a retired Navy SEAL.
- Charles "Chuck" and Marie Sawyer: Ian, Devon, and Nick's parents. Charles is a self-made real estate billionaire. Marie is a plastic surgeon involved with Operation Smile.
- Will Anders: Assistant Curator of the Tampa Museum of Art Kristen Anders's cousin.

- Dr. Roxanne London: pediatrician; Domme/wife (Mistress Roxy) of Kayla; Whip Master at Covenant.
- Kayla London: social worker; submissive/wife of Roxanne.
- Grayson and Remington Mann: twins; owners of Black Diamond Records; Doms/fiancés of Abigail; members of The Covenant.
- Abigail Turner: personal assistant at Black Diamond Records; submissive/fiancée of Gray and Remi.
- Chase Dixon: retired Marine Raider; owner of Blackhawk Security; associate of TS.
- Reggie Helm: lawyer for TS and The Covenant; Dom/husband of Colleen.
- Alyssa Wagner: teenager saved by Jake from an abusive father; lives with Rick and Eileen Michaelson.
- Dr. Trudy Dunbar: Psychologist.
- Carl Talbot: college professor; Dom and Whip Master at The Covenant.

The Omega Team and Their Significant Others

- Cain Foster: retired Secret Service agent.
- Tristan "Duracell" McCabe: retired Army Special Forces

- Valentino "Romeo" Mancini: retired Army Special Forces; former FBI Hostage Rescue Team (HRT) member.
- Darius "Batman" Knight: retired Navy SEAL.
- Kip "Skipper" Morrison: retired Army; former LAPD SWAT sniper.
- Lindsey "Costello" Abbott: retired Marine; sniper.

Trident Support Staff

- Colleen McKinley-Helm: office manager of TS; wife/submissive of Reggie.
- Tempest "Babs" Van Buren: retired Air Force helicopter pilot; TS mechanic.
- Russell Adams: retired Navy; assistant TS mechanic.
- Nathan Cook: former computer specialist with the National Security Agency (NSA).

Members of Law Enforcement

- Larry Keon: Assistant Director of the FBI.
- Frank Stonewall: Special Agent in Charge of the Tampa FBI.
- Calvin Watts: Leader of the FBI HRT in Tampa.

The K9s of Trident

- Beau: An orphaned Lab/Pit mix, rescued by Ian. Now a trained K9 who has more than earned his spot on the Alpha Team.
- Spanky: A rescued Bullmastiff with a heart of gold, owned by Parker and Shelby.
- Jagger: A rescued Rottweiler trained as an assistance/service animal for Russell.

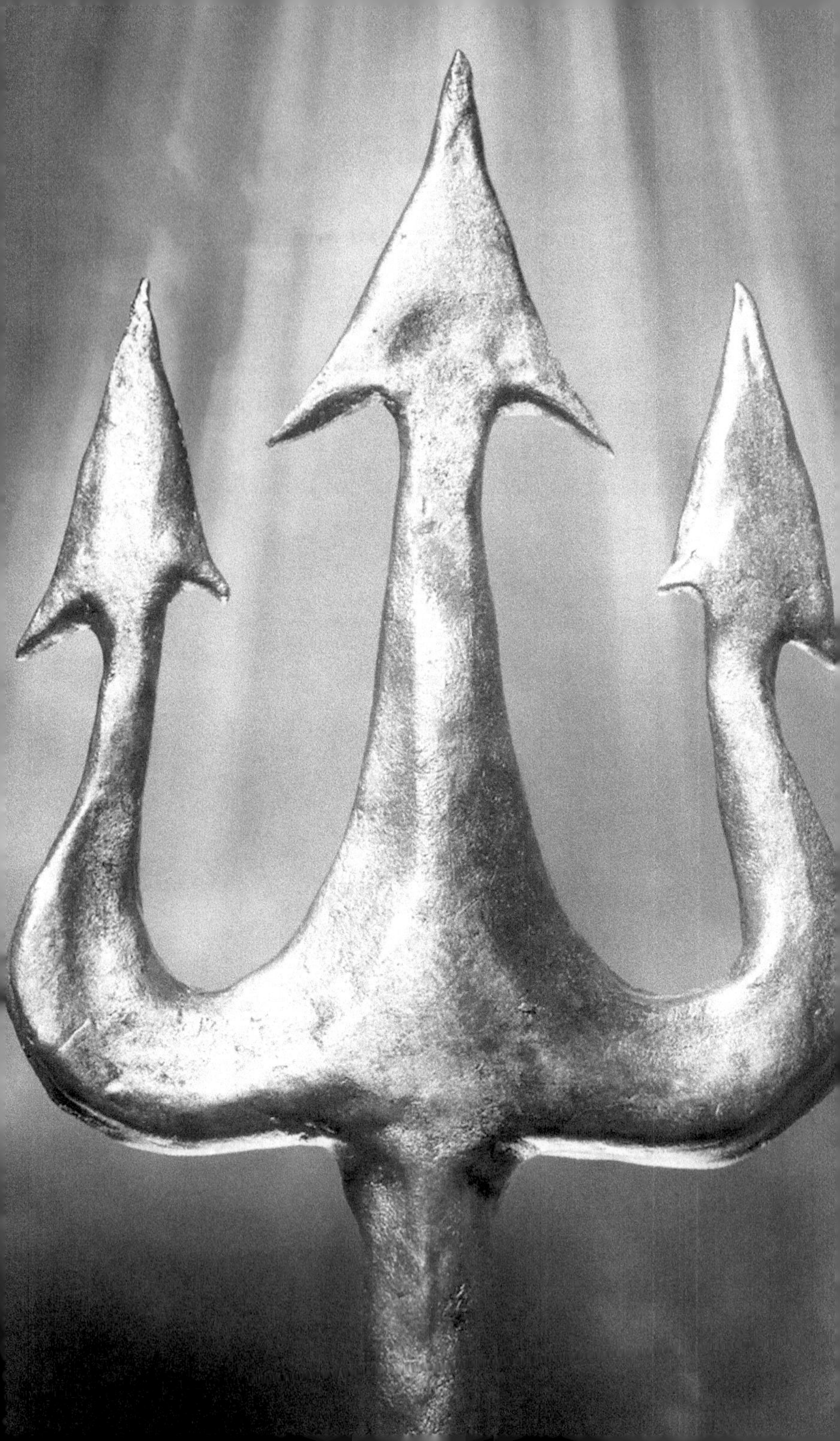

CHAPTER ONE

Mitch Sawyer slammed his laptop closed. He was working on next month's schedule for his employees and the Dungeon Monitors but found it hard to concentrate. He had no idea why he was so stressed—everything was going great at the BDSM club he owned with his cousins, Ian and Devon. The new wing had opened in time for their Christmas party, and they had a ribbon-cutting ceremony before showing off The Covenant's dome-covered garden.

His gaze flitted to the photos in an array on his wall. Some were from when they'd been renovating, while others were from special events they'd held over the years. This elite club in Tampa, Florida, was his baby—more so than his cousins'. When the idea of opening it had come to him, his MBA had come in handy. Leaving the company he'd been working for, The Covenant became his full-time job, managing it while his cousins tended to their other business, Trident Security. Six years later, it was the thriving business he'd hoped it would be.

Taking a deep breath, he forced it out again. He had to get some playtime in tonight. That would settle him—it usually did. Maybe a new submissive from the class that finished training last month would be willing to negotiate a scene with him tonight. Yeah, that definitely held numerous possibilities, which made his day brighter.

A knock sounded at his office door as he opened his laptop again. He glanced at the clock: 5:07 p.m., less than an hour before the doors opened for the night. "Come in," he said.

The door swung open, and Mitch's dick twitched when he saw who was standing there and what she was wearing. Tori Freyja had been a submissive member of the club for the past six months. She'd joined after she'd helped Russell Adams, a Navy veteran who'd been an integral part in saving Brody Evans's life. Brody was one of the employees of Trident Security, having been on the same SEAL Team as Ian and Dev. He'd been kidnapped by the guy who'd been obsessed with his now fiancée, Fancy Maguire. Russell had been stabbed during the attack but had held on to consciousness long enough to let Ian and the police know what'd happened. After he'd recovered from surgery, Ian introduced him to Tori. Sweet, sexy, submissive Tori.

The introduction had nothing to do with romance or the lifestyle and everything to do with what Tori did for a living. She trained service/assistance dogs for veterans with PTSD or who had sustained a disabling physical injury during combat, as well as children with autism. She was also involved in a Bullmastiff rescue and had placed one of the big dogs with another club Dom, Parker Christiansen. After Russell was released from the hospital, he'd gone to Tori's ranch just north of Tampa, where he helped train the dog that was going to help him when he had flashbacks or bouts of depression.

And now Tori had been granted a free membership. Well, it hadn't exactly been free—Ian had paid for it. He'd said it was the least he could do for a woman doing so much to help veterans deal with the day-to-day repercussions of their tours of duty. Ian was a hard-ass most of the time, but deep down, he had a soft heart. Falling in love with his wife had just made that softness rise to the surface more often.

"Good evening, Master Mitch. I don't mean to disturb you, but I wanted to ask you something, and Master Dennis asked me to give you the bar inventory list since I was headed back here."

She held up several pieces of white paper, but his gaze wasn't on them. Instead, he was drinking her in. With long, wavy, dark-blonde hair and brown eyes, she stood five foot six, and he guessed she was a size 12 or 14. He loved women with Marilyn Monroe curves.

Her club wear for the night was a black bustier with a pattern of white skulls and swirls on it. A matching pair of panties and black thigh-highs completed the erotic look. She had simple, black slippers on her feet, which many submissives wore unless told otherwise by their Doms. They weren't necessary in the pit as the floor was cleaned every other day, and no drinks other than plastic water bottles were allowed there. Many Doms preferred their submissives in bare feet, and this way they didn't have to worry about broken glass or anything that might cut them. As for the garden, there was soft, faux grass in there, so, again, it was safe for the subs.

Staring at her, he was grateful he was sitting behind the desk and she couldn't see his growing hard-on. He'd been interested in playing with her after she completed her submissive training, but he'd waited too long, and another Dom had snatched her up. "Come in, Tori. You may have a seat."

"Thank you, Sir." She placed the papers on the desk in front of him, then gracefully lowered herself into one of the two guest chairs.

"You're here early. Where's Master Tyler?" Tyler Ellis, a bisexual stockbroker, had signed a contract with the pretty submissive about three months ago. The majority of the time, he was a Dom to female submissives, but he was known in the club as a switch and sometimes sought out a male Dominant to give him the flipside of a power exchange. Before Mitch's younger cousin Nick had gotten into a committed relationship with Ian and Dev's teammate, Jake Donovan, Tyler and Jake had scened together occasionally.

"Sir had a business meeting after the market closed, so I came in with Cassandra. He'll be here later, and we'll follow her home at the end of her shift. Master Stefan is working this weekend."

Cassandra Myers was one of the club's submissives who waitressed several nights per week. In addition to her generous pay and tips, she was granted play rights when she wasn't working, and Mitch was glad to hear she already had an escort home later since her Dom wouldn't be here. For over seven months now, a serial killer had been targeting submissive women in the lifestyle and torturing them with a bullwhip before killing them and dumping their bodies. Public and private BDSM clubs within a hundred-mile radius had been on high alert and doing what they could to ensure their submissives' safety. However, no matter what security measures they took, it hadn't been enough to prevent ten women from being viciously murdered. Most of them had disappeared following an evening of playing at a club. One of the mandatory policies Ian, Devon, and Mitch had put in place at The Covenant in response to the slayings was no female submissive went home without an escort. If they weren't under contract with a Dom, then either the Dom they'd played with that night or one of the Dungeon Masters or security personnel followed them home. All the Doms had been stepping up to help with the single subs.

"Good. Then what was your question?" Mitch scratched the coarse hair covering his jaw. He'd stopped shaving a few weeks ago, as he did every once in a while, just because it was tiresome to do every morning. In another few weeks, he'd get tired of the beard and mustache and get rid of them again.

Her cheeks blushed, spiking his curiosity. But like a good submissive, she held his gaze while in conversation. If they were scening or following club protocol, her gaze would be shifted downward unless otherwise told by the Dom she was interacting with. "Um... well, I was wondering if I could ask you for a favor. Please don't feel like you have to say yes, but I was wondering if you wouldn't mind going to Vegas with Tyler and me this weekend." Mitch arched an eyebrow at her but let her continue. "There's a wedding in my family. My cousin, Celia, is getting married, and our other cousin, Tiffany, is also in the lifestyle. She was in a contracted relationship for over a year, but it recently ended. Thank God. Her Master wasn't a good one, and I think he's in the lifestyle for all the wrong reasons. He didn't treat her right, and I was glad they broke up. But the problem is that Bruce is friends with the groom and will also be at the wedding. While she could probably bring someone who isn't a Dom, she'd feel better with one. And none of the Doms in her club will come between them and escort her. It's a public club in

Vegas, and I hate that she goes there—it's not safe. Anyway, I hoped you'd be willing to take her to the wedding. She's really sweet and a lot of fun. Whether you negotiate with her or not is up to you two. I'll pay for your flight and room and—"

Mitch held up his hand. "Stop right there, Tori. If I agree to go, there is no way I'm letting you pay for anything for me. I'm very capable of paying my own way." In addition to the club, Mitch had invested well—through Tyler's company and with his uncle's business advice. Devon and Ian's father, Mitch's Uncle Chuck, was a self-made real estate billionaire, and as a result, the rest of the family had reaped the benefits of Charles Sawyer's savvy mind.

Her gaze dropped to the desk. "I'm sorry. I didn't mean to insult you or imply anything, Sir."

"You didn't, Tori. Look at me." Her eyes lifted again. "How old is Tiffany?"

"Twenty-seven. Three years younger than me, Sir."

And seven years younger than Mitch. That was doable. He couldn't believe he was considering going to a wedding in Vegas. It wasn't that he hated weddings. They were just a reminder that everyone else around him was falling in love and getting married, but he'd yet to find a woman he was willing to spend the rest of his life with, much less a few months. However, if he stayed in Tampa this coming weekend, he'd be subjected to another reminder anyway. Ian and his wife Angie were throwing a barbecue in Ian's Oasis, as the "backyard" between the last two buildings in the Trident Security compound had been dubbed. Angie was pregnant, and they were celebrating the announcement and the return of Ben "Boomer" and Kat Michaelson from their honeymoon. "How long has she been in the lifestyle?"

"Five years, Sir."

"Did she approve of you asking me to escort her?"

Tori nodded. "Yes, Sir. I wouldn't have asked you if it wasn't okay with her."

"Was her Dom abusive?"

"I'm not one hundred percent sure because Tiffany always denied it, but yes, I think he was verbally, emotionally, and physically abusive to her."

That settled it. There was nothing he loved more than putting a cruel asshole in his place. "I'd be honored to take her. Please have her call me tomorrow to talk before I meet her. What's the flight itinerary?"

A smile had spread across Tori's face when he'd agreed to take the trip, and it felt like he'd gotten kicked in the gut. How was he supposed to survive a weekend in Vegas with Tori when he couldn't have her for himself? But he'd already said yes and couldn't disappoint her and back out now.

"We're flying out on Friday morning and returning on Monday morning. Sir and I decided to stay an extra day to have some fun that's not wedding-related. It's been a while since either of us was in Vegas. I'll have him email you our flight and hotel information when we get home tonight so you can book yours. And thank you so much, Sir."

"It'll be my pleasure, pet. Oh, what's the dress code for the wedding? In Vegas, it can range from lingerie and surf shorts to animal costumes to black tie."

Her giggle was adorable. "Master Tyler is wearing a suit, and I'm wearing a dress, if that helps, Sir."

"Then I'll bring a suit as well. Is there anything else you need?"

She obviously understood she was being dismissed because she stood. Mitch was reluctant to let her go, but with her rocking that bustier, he was hard as granite, and the black leather collar around her neck said she was off limits. "No, Sir. That's it. And thank you again, Sir. It means a lot to me, especially since it's with little notice."

"No worries, Tori. Now, let me finish up here so I can make it onto the club floor sometime this evening."

"Yes, Sir."

When she turned and sashayed toward the door, Mitch bit back a groan. She was as hot going as she was coming. His head dropped against the back of the soft leather chair as Tori disappeared into the hallway.

Damn, I need to get laid tonight.

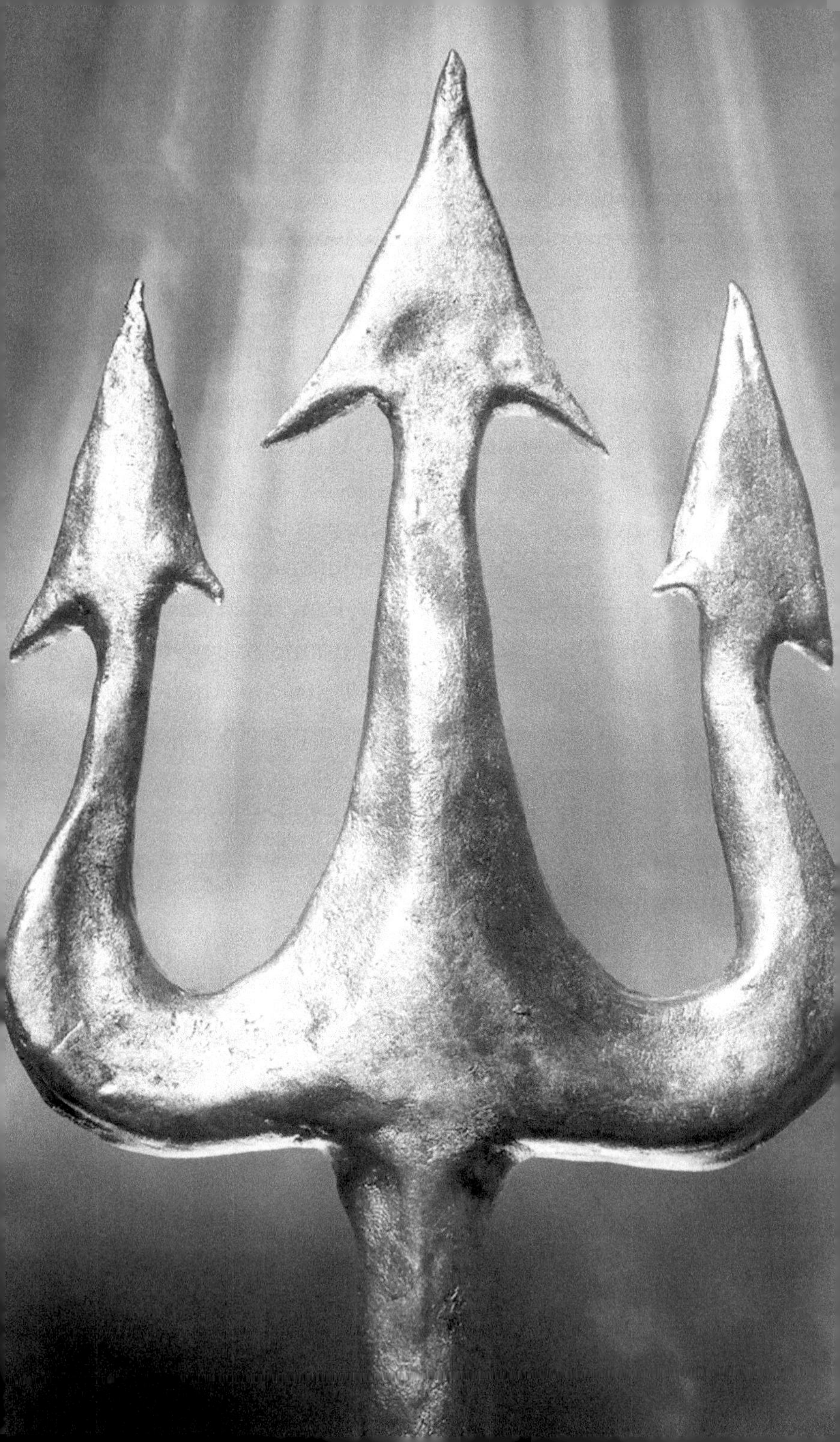

CHAPTER TWO

As Tori headed for the club's bar for ginger ale to settle her stomach, she let out the breath she'd been holding since she stood and felt Master Mitch's eyes on her ass as she walked out of his office. She'd felt his eyes on her ass the entire way. Why he made her blood run as hot as it did with Tyler was beyond her. But during the whole conversation, her nipples had been hard, her clit had throbbed, and her pussy had been weeping for the man's cock to fill her.

She loved Tyler, of that she was sure. So why did her body crave another man? Maybe she'd talk to Tyler about a threesome with Mitch sometime. Perhaps that would get him out of her system. While Tyler was bisexual, which she didn't have a problem with as long as she was involved, Mitch was straight. She wasn't sure if he would be into a ménage with a bi even though they didn't have to be intimate with each other. While in the lifestyle for a few years, she was still relatively new to The Covenant and hadn't learned everyone's kinks, quirks, and preferences.

The black-haired co-owner and manager of the club had caught her eye during her first training class, which he'd taught. Whether previously in the lifestyle or not, all Doms and submissives were required to take the basic introduction classes before being approved for play. The advanced classes were optional unless the person was a complete newbie to BDSM, and she'd been tempted to take them anyway so that she could drool over the head instructor. But she discovered through the grapevine that Master Mitch didn't play with new club members, experienced or not, for at least a few months after they were approved. None of the submissives she'd spoken to knew why. After Master Tyler first expressed interest in a contract with her, she'd pushed the other Dom to the back of her mind. However, her body didn't seem to want to keep him there. And now she would be spending an entire weekend with him, so to speak.

Reaching the bar area again, she realized she still had time to kill before other club members poured in. Cassandra and the other waitresses, the bartender, and security were getting ready for the Sunday night crowd, and Tori would just be in their way, so she hurried back down to the women's locker room where she'd changed earlier. It hadn't been necessary for her to put her fet-wear on before going to Mitch's office, but for some reason, she'd wanted to. The heat she'd seen in his eyes when she first walked in had been worth it, but then it disappeared, and the conversation had become business-like. But that momentary flash of desire she'd detected had been enough to set her heart pounding.

After opening her locker, she retrieved her phone and took the stairs back up to the lobby. Cell phone use and cameras were prohibited on the club floor and in the locker rooms unless given specific permission from the owners, which was rare. All calls and texts had to be taken in the lobby or the parking lot, which helped ensure the members' privacy.

With a brief wave toward where Travis "Tiny" Daultry, the head of club security, and Matthew, a male submissive who ran the front desk, were chatting, Tori sat on one of the lobby's sofas and turned on her phone. Scrolling through her contacts, she called Russell Adams. That afternoon, he'd had a flashback after a low-flying helicopter had buzzed the ranch. Thankfully, his new assistance dog, Jagger, whom he'd been training for the last few months, had done exactly what he was supposed to do. The Rottweiler had made circles around Russell, creating a comfort barrier for his human while nudging him toward a bale of hay to sit on. He then put his big head in the man's lap, licking his hands to bring him back to the present. The dog stayed like that until the flashback ended and Russell's breathing and heart rate had returned to normal, and his body had stopped trembling.

Despite the ranch's staff being experienced with PTSD, the vets tended to be embarrassed after an incident, and Russell was no exception. She didn't want him to think she was checking up on him, so she'd go with a red herring.

"Hello?"

"Hi, Russell, it's Tori." She tried to keep the concern out of her voice. "Can you do me a favor when you get a chance?"

"Um... sure."

"Great. I hoped I'd return in time, but that won't happen. Can you go help Jasmine with feeding the puppies tonight?" The other trainer and Tori had set this up in advance. All Russell had to do was go from his bunkhouse to the kennel where seven four-week-old Labrador/mix pups were being bottle-fed since their mother had been hit by a car and killed a few days after giving birth. They would start being weaned toward the end of the week. A local police officer had been called to the scene by the distraught driver, and they heard crying and yelps coming from a storm drain. The three males and four females were then transported to the veterinarian Tori used. After giving them flea baths and clean bills of health, she'd called Healing Heroes to see if they could foster them and possibly turn them into assistance dogs. All the dogs that Tori's non-profit organization trained were rescues. They also trained police and security dogs to offset expenses when donations were down.

"Um... yeah, sure. Is it okay for me to bring Jagger with me? Or are they still in quarantine?"

"They haven't gotten their vaccinations yet, but you can bring Jagger since he's all up-to-date with his own shots. Just have him stay across the room. Jasmine knows what to do." Tori suspected the veteran had a thing for her business partner, and Jazz had already confided she was attracted to him but thought it was best to become friends with him first before cluing him in.

"Great. And... uh... I'm really sorry about—"

She cut him off, her voice gentle with understanding. "There's nothing to be sorry about, Russell. You're not the first vet who's had an episode at the ranch, and I'm sure you won't be the last. That's the whole point of you being there with Jagger. I'm not sure if you noticed, but your episodes are less frequent now than when you first came to us."

"Really?" He paused. "You know, you may be right. I hadn't realized it."

Tori laughed. "That's because we've been working your ass off. You've been too preoccupied to notice."

"Maybe. Listen. I know I've said this a hundred times since I got out of the hospital, but thanks again, Tori, for all you've done for me... and for the other vets. It means more to us than you'll ever know."

A lump formed in her throat, and she swallowed it

down. "It's been my pleasure. Tell Jazz I'll see her tomorrow. And have fun with the pups."

"I will. Have a good night."

"Thanks."

Disconnecting the call, Tori smiled. *Damn, I love my job.*

Tyler Ellis pulled into the club parking lot and found a spot for his BMW convertible. The after-hours staff meeting had gone longer than expected, and he'd shot a text off to Matthew, who was manning the front desk of The Covenant, to pass on the delay to Tori. He didn't want her to worry, and her cell phone would be in her locker.

He was seriously jonesing to be topped tonight. While he was madly in love with his submissive, Tori, there were times *he* needed to submit to another male Dom. The urge was most potent when he was stressed. Thankfully, he'd found a woman who was willing to accept that he was a bisexual switch. In fact, she loved to watch and occasionally joined in the scene if the Dom was willing to top both of them simultaneously.

There were a few gay or bisexual Doms who he'd scened with over the past few years. Jake Donovan had been one of his favorites—the guy was hot and a Whip Master at the club. But since Jake had fallen in love and collared Ian and Devon Sawyer's brother, Nick, he'd been unavailable to scene with other men. Even if he was still on the market, he'd temporarily relocated to California while his sub completed his final tour with the Navy. They were planning a summer wedding in Tampa after getting engaged at Christmas.

If a gay or bisexual Dom wasn't available to scene, Tyler turned to the other Whip Masters at the club for a session with a bullwhip. Vanilla people might think he was crazy, begging to be whipped across his back, buttocks, and thighs, but that's how he was wired. It was how he could let go of all the stress that came with being a stockbroker.

Grabbing his duffel bag, he climbed out of the car and strode toward the stairs leading to the second-floor entrance. The new wing had increased the club's size by at least fifty percent. The added theme rooms were great, but everyone loved the new garden. During the grand opening, Mitch Sawyer compared it to Eden, and no one disagreed with him.

Damn. Just thinking of the sexy, black-haired Dom had Tyler's cock twitching in his dress pants. It fucking sucked the guy was straight because Tyler would love to get his hands on that drool-worthy body.

Stepping into the lobby, Tyler swallowed hard. The masculine object of his recent fantasies was standing at the front desk, talking with Matthew. Tyler subtly drank him in. The man wore his brown leather pants and boots tonight, with a snug, tan T-shirt that outlined his fine physique. His hair was a little long at the collar, and combined with his current facial hair, it made him look a few years younger than thirty-four, a year older than Tyler.

Heading toward the double doors separating the lobby from the bar area, Tyler was surprised when Mitch caught his eye and waved him over as he stepped away from the desk.

"Evening, Mitch. What's up?" Most of the time, he identified as a Dom and, as such, didn't need to follow submissive protocols unless negotiating or performing a scene with another Dom. Since he was doing neither of those things, he didn't have to avert his gaze or call Mitch Master or Sir.

"Hey, Ty. Looks like I'll be joining you and Tori in Vegas this weekend. She was going to have you send me the flight info so I can see if a seat is available."

Tyler's jaw dropped. "Really?"

"Yeah." Mitch's eyes narrowed. "Problem? Tori didn't tell you she was asking me?"

"No! No problem at all. And she told me she was going to ask you, but I didn't think you'd be up to going on such late notice."

The man shrugged. "No big deal. Gets me out of a family thing this weekend with all the wedding and baby announcements. At least in Vegas, I can avoid chatter about bridesmaid dresses, Lamaze classes, or babies shitting their diapers."

A chuckle escaped Tyler. "Not your cup of tea, huh?"

"I don't know. Maybe when I get to that point in my life, I'll be the same way and happy about it. Now, I kind of feel like a sixth toe."

"I hear ya." He had to get away from Mitch. The combination of the man's cologne and unique scent drove Tyler crazy. If he couldn't handle a two-minute conversation with the guy, how the hell would he get through a whole weekend with him? *Shit!*

"Listen. I called my Uncle Chuck, and if you two are interested, no one's using his company's penthouse at The Mirage for the entire weekend, so I booked it. It's got two bedrooms, a living room, a kitchen, the works. You're welcome to save some money and bunk there with me."

"Uh... yeah. I guess. As long as we're not intruding." *Fuck. Fuck. Fuck.*

Mitch slapped him on the shoulder and started walking toward the double doors. "Not at all. The place is great and has plenty of room."

Tyler's mind and body were in turmoil as he followed the other man. *What the hell have I gotten myself into?*

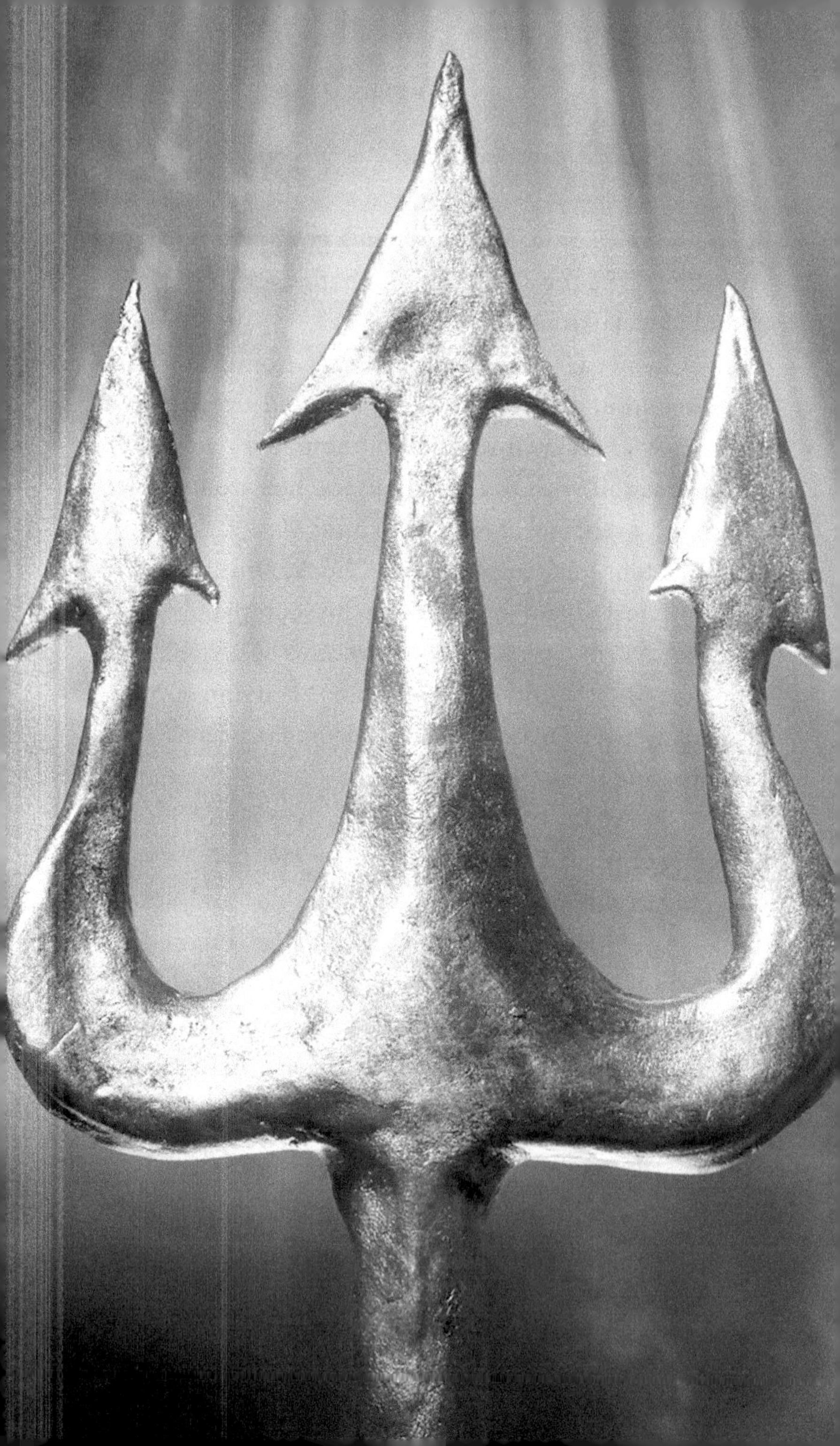

CHAPTER THREE

"Blackjack! Congratulations, sir!"

Mitch grinned as he tossed a twenty-five-dollar chip toward the pretty Asian dealer for giving him the $250 hand. "Thanks."

"Jeez. What do you have that I don't?" Tyler grumbled, staring at the two cards in front of him, which totaled fourteen against the house's jack of diamonds up card. "That's the third one she's given you in twenty minutes."

He winked at the dealer. "It's my charm, charisma, and good looks. Right, Mika?"

"Absolutely, sir," she responded with a flirtatious smile.

After landing at the airport three hours ago, they checked into their suite and then met Tori's cousin, Tiffany, in the steakhouse for a late dinner. Now, the two ladies were at a row of slot machines just behind where Mitch and Tyler were playing on the high-stakes tables. Tiffany squealed loudly a few minutes ago when she'd hit four aces for eight hundred dollars.

His date for tomorrow's wedding was a sweet woman but a bit jittery and wary. She was definitely a submissive, but after reassuring her he wasn't big on high protocol, especially outside of a club or scene setting, she seemed to relax more. Her ex-Dom must have done a number on her. From what Mitch had been able to figure out during dinner, their relationship seemed to be that of a Dom/slave instead of a Dom/submissive one. There was a considerable difference between the two. Slaves tended to rely on their Doms to make all their decisions for them—from what to wear and eat to anything and everything else that was in their contract. Mitch wasn't sure Tiffany had been happy as a slave—she may have just agreed to it because that's what the dickhead Dom had wanted.

While perusing the menus, Tiffany kept glancing at him whenever she said a dish sounded delicious, probably waiting for him to approve or disapprove of her choice. Ultimately, he'd taken her menu from her, then held her hand and had her close her eyes. Once she did, he asked what dish was the first to pop into her head. After blurting out "salmon," she opened her eyes and smiled at him. It would take some reconditioning, preferably under a new and caring Dom, but she would recover from the bad relationship. In the meantime, Mitch looked forward to meeting the bastard tomorrow night—he had some choice words and maybe a fist or two for the guy if they were ever alone.

While Mitch liked Tiffany—she was pretty and shapely—he couldn't help his body's reaction to her cousin. Tori simply had to laugh, and it went straight to his groin. Maybe she and Tyler would be interested in a threesome this weekend. He'd been in several ménages over the years, but they were always for a night or weekend—nothing more. He and Tyler could top Tori together, which might get her out of Mitch's system. He'd play it by ear.

As the dealer shuffled the cards, Mitch glanced over his shoulder and froze. Tori and Tiffany were surrounded by three college guys who'd obviously had one too many. Despite the women trying to ignore them, the idiots were getting a little touchy-feely— and even a little was too much for Mitch. "Hey, Ty..."

Standing, he didn't wait for the other man to respond, knowing he'd be right behind him. Mitch closed the distance to the group just in time to hear the tall, blond dickhead on the right say, "Come on, babes. We'll show you a really good time. Dressed like that, you know you want it."

Mitch's growl was in tandem with Tyler's. He grabbed the asshole's wrist, pulled his hand away from where it'd been rubbing Tiffany's bare shoulder, and dug his thumb into a pressure point. It was a trick he'd learned from his Navy SEAL cousins. Blondie glared at him, then winced as the pain penetrated his alcohol-fuzzed brain. The guy was obviously a gym rat or a lunkhead, like in those commercials for Planet Fitness. Just because your muscles bulged didn't mean you knew how to use them. "Hey, get the fuck off, man!"

"That's my line. That's my woman you're touching, asshole." Technically, she wasn't, but for the weekend, he was her Dom, whether or not sex was involved, and she was his responsibility.

Beside him, Tyler got between the other two drunks and Tori, and the idiots weren't happy about it. They started throwing out derogatory insults and demanded to know if Tyler wanted to fight. He might be an inch shorter than Mitch's six foot even, but he was in excellent shape for a desk jockey. Mitch wasn't worried about Ty, but he *was* worried about Tori and Tiffany—the five men sort of blocked them in. Both women stood and spun around, ready to run if punches were thrown, but Mitch didn't want to escalate things. The night had been going great, and he didn't want to ruin it by getting kicked out of the casino. It was a good thing he flew to Vegas a few times a year with Dev, Ian, and the rest of the Trident boys because when security rushed over, a few recognized Mitch right away.

"Problem, Mr. Sawyer?" The six-foot-four, broad-shouldered supervisor spoke in a low but commanding voice, his gaze focused on the three drunks.

Letting go of the other guy's wrist, he shook his head and read the man's nameplate. "Not if these idiots walk away, Darrell."

"Fuck you, dickhead," blondie sneered.

Mitch smirked. "You're not my type, asshole. But maybe one of your buddies is willing to suck your steroid shrinkage."

Aaaaaand here it comes... The jerk swung, but his arm was stopped short by two security guards, one of whom could be a distant cousin of The Covenant's head of security, Tiny Daultry, a former professional football player. Within seconds, they escorted the three drunks out of the casino. Most people in the area had no idea the incident had gone down, the blaring slot machines muting most conversation.

Turning back to the supervisor, Mitch shook his hand. "Sorry about that, Darrell."

"No worries, Mr. Sawyer. Ladies, are you okay?"

Tiffany nodded, clearly still shaken up, while Tori responded, "Yes. We're fine, thank you."

"My pleasure. If you need anything, let me know, and I'll have it taken care of."

With a nod of his head, the man disappeared into the crowd. Mitch eyed Tiffany—she was pale and trembling. He took her hand and rubbed his thumb over the back of it. "Why don't we call it a night? I'll drive your car to your place, then take a cab back here."

Her eyes went wide. "Y-you don't have to do that, Ma... I mean, Mitch. I can drive home by myself. I don't want you to go out of your way."

"You're my responsibility tonight, Tiffany, and I won't take no for an answer. I'll take you home, call a cab to meet me there, and make sure you're safely inside before coming back here." He wanted her to understand he wasn't expecting anything for escorting her to her condo in the suburbs of Vegas. "If you're more comfortable with Tori and Tyler coming with us, I'm sure they won't mind."

Tiffany's tense shoulders eased. "Um... no, that's... that's not necessary. I trust you." She took the receipt of her winnings from Tori. "Thank you. I just need to cash this in, if that's okay, Sir?"

He didn't want to correct her use of the word Sir in this setting since it would probably make her uncomfortable, so he let it slide. "Perfectly okay. Let me and Ty get our chips from the table, and we can all cash in."

"Except for me," Tori pouted. "I lost forty dollars."

Grinning, Tyler pulled her into his arms. "That's all right, babe. I'll make it up to you tonight."

Forty-five minutes later, Mitch rode the private elevator up to their penthouse suite. It was still early —just 11:30 p.m.—but it'd been a long day, and his bed sounded like heaven. He stepped into the opulent foyer when the doors slid open and stopped short. *Shit.* Ty and Tori were going at it in the living room, and from the sound of it, she was nearing an orgasm.

Mitch's cock hardened. He didn't even have to see her—just hearing her begging and moaning was enough to do him in. There was no way he could get to his bedroom without walking right past them—not that it wasn't something he didn't see nightly at the club.

"Please, Sir! Oh, please!"

"Not yet, little subbie. You can hold off a little longer."

Yeah, but I can't. Before he did something stupid, like walk into the living room and sit down to watch, Mitch turned on his heel and hit the elevator call button. Thankfully, the car was still on their floor, and the doors opened immediately. Boarding, he pressed the button for the casino.

Just as the doors shut, he heard Tyler say, "Come for me, Tori."

And fuck... she did.

Ty's fingers caressed Tori's upper arm as she cuddled into his side. His mind was spinning and each time it stopped, it landed on the man who'd returned to the suite about fifteen minutes ago—just after 2:00 a.m.

Being attracted to both men and women was sometimes a curse, and this was one of those times. He loved the naked woman in his arms, but he lusted after a man he couldn't have.

"What're you thinking about?" Tori stirred and found a more comfortable spot on his shoulder to lay her head. Her fingers traced the contours of his chest and his few tattoos there.

For the first time in their relationship, Ty lied to her. "About you."

"Mmm. What about me?"

He took a deep breath, then rubbed his week-old beard against her hair. "What do you think about asking Mitch to join us some time as a third? He's definitely interested in you. I caught him watching you a few times tonight. Be honest."

"I'm always honest with you." After he'd just told her a fib, he felt as if he'd gotten punched in the gut when she said that. Tori tilted her head so she could see his face. "I like Mitch. He's nice, good-looking, and caring. I wouldn't mind him being a third." She paused. "Would you mind?"

"Not at all." Ty stared across the room at nothing in particular.

"You're attracted to him, aren't you?"

His gaze shot to hers. He shouldn't be shocked she'd been able to see through his pitiful façade, but he was. Worried he'd hurt her, he was relieved to see understanding in her eyes. "I love you. That will never change. I think I fell in love with you the moment I saw you. But you're right. I am attracted to him." Her caramel-brown eyes heated, and he raised his hand to caress her cheek. "You're attracted to him too, hmm?"

"Yes. But I'm in love with you, so please don't be worried about that. If you can't have a third in our relationship who you want, neither can I. Yes, we're both attracted to him, but we can wait until we find someone willing to top us both, okay?"

God, he loved her. Rolling her onto her back, he settled his hips between her thighs. "That's more than okay, baby."

His lips descended onto hers as his straining erection found her pussy wet and waiting for him. Thankfully, Tori was on the birth control shot, and both of them had recently had their required physicals for The Covenant because he loved taking her without a condom. His tongue delved into her mouth, dancing with hers as he thrust his hips forward. Her body yielded to his entry as if it had been made explicitly for him. Slow and easy was the pace he set. Earlier, they'd fucked like rabbits on the couch, but right now, he didn't want to fuck her—he wanted to make love to her. To show her how much she meant to him.

Leaving her mouth, Ty kissed her chin and jawline, his beard rasping against her skin. Her hands were clenching the pillow on either side of her head like a good little subbie, waiting for her Master's command.

"Touch me, Tori. Free reign this time. I want to feel your hands on me."

Caressing his arms and shoulders, she explored every inch of him. Her fingers curved inward, and he felt the bite of her manicured nails. A groan escaped him. He loved it when she scratched his flesh. It was her way of marking him and the only pain he'd allow her to give him. When he needed more, he turned to a Dom for a round of lashes with a bullwhip or flogger. He'd tried it a few times with a Domme but hadn't received the same level of satisfaction and euphoria he got with other men. There was probably some sort of psychological or biological reason for it, but Ty didn't care. It was what worked for him.

As Tori dragged her nails across his skin, Ty tucked his hands under her lush ass, tilting her hips. The new position allowed him to sink further into her heat with each inward stroke. The drag of her walls lit up every nerve in his stiff cock. Hooking an arm under her knee, he lifted it toward her torso. And damn, that felt even better. He gave his hips a slight twist to get a better angle, then increased the intensity and pace of his thrusts. A gasp followed by a deep moan told him he'd hit her G-spot dead-on. His pelvis hit her clit over and over, sending her higher. He was so close to coming but wanted her to go first.

"Come for me, baby." Lifting her knee a little further so he could reach her nipple, his fingers closed around the taut nub and pinched.

Tori's shriek of pure ecstasy bounced off the walls of their bedroom as her pussy clenched and quivered around him. Ty's eyes slammed shut as his own orgasm followed, and he poured his seed deep inside her. "*Ahhh... ffffuuuccckk!*"

Letting her leg go, Ty's head hit the pillow next to hers as he kept most of his weight on his pelvis and forearms. He didn't want to leave her heat until he had to. He kissed and nibbled on her ear as she basked in the afterglow of their coupling. "I love you, pet."

As exhaustion overtook her, she murmured, "I love you too, Sir."

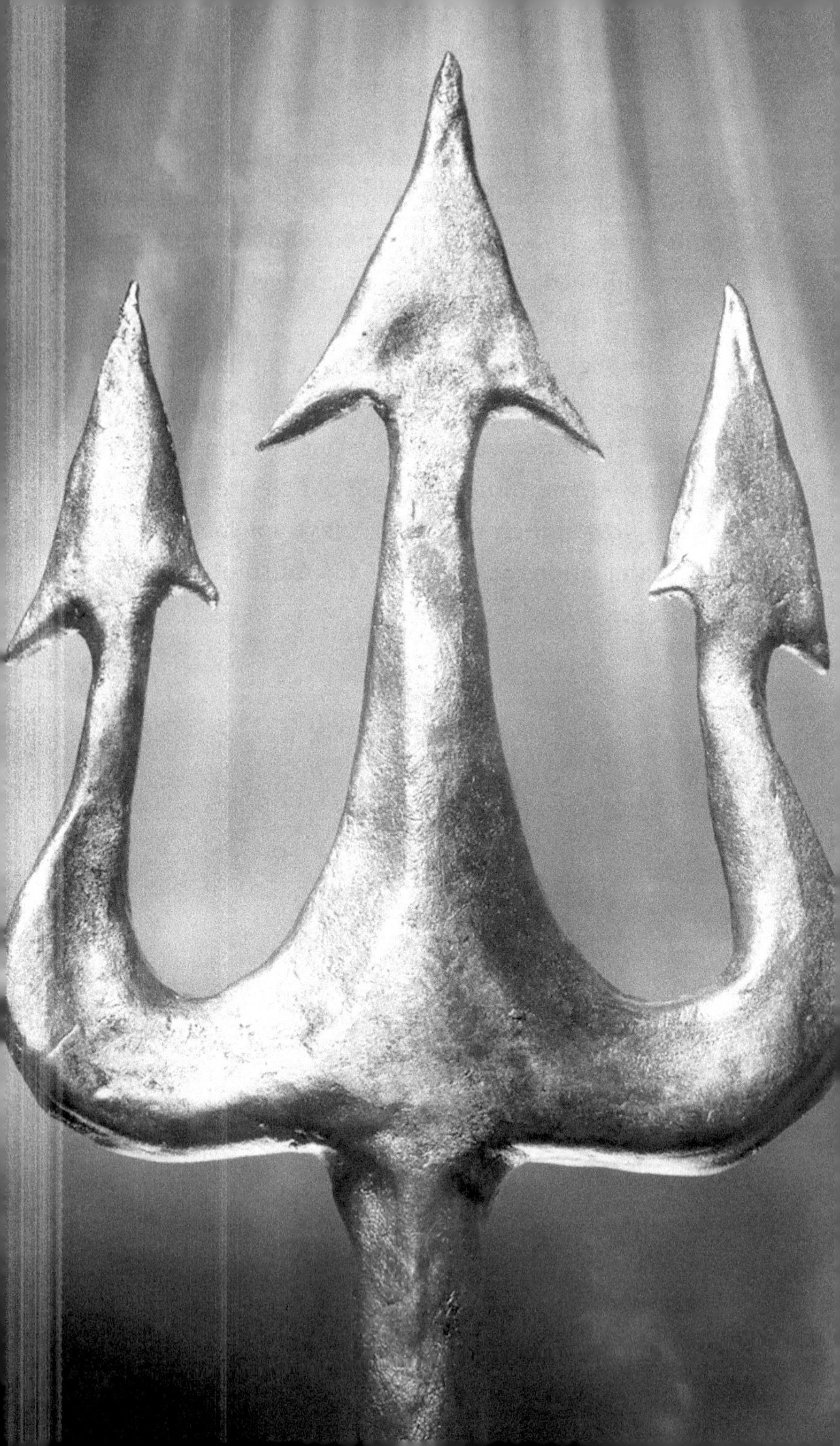

CHAPTER FOUR

Walking into the banquet hall of the Red Rock Country Club, Mitch's mind was still spinning. Ian had called him a few hours ago and told him one of The Covenant's Doms had been interrogated by the FBI in connection with the serial killings, and neither Mitch nor his cousins could believe it. The Dom was released after two hours, mainly because Reggie Helm had refused to let his new client answer any questions that might incriminate him. Without a court order, the lawyer wouldn't allow a DNA sample to be taken, but that would, no doubt, be coming soon. The issue Ian was pissed about was that the Dom stated he wouldn't name the submissive woman who could provide him with alibis for at least two of the killings. Apparently, it would jeopardize her career, whatever it was. For now, the Dom wasn't under arrest, but that would change unless new evidence cleared him. Mitch hoped the lead FBI investigator, Special Agent Colt Parrish, was wrong in assuming the guy was guilty.

With Tori and Ty joining them, Mitch led Tiffany to the bar, his hand splayed across her back in reassurance. Her ex hadn't been at the ceremony earlier but would be there for the reception, and the sub was nervous as hell. This would be the first time she'd see him since moving out of his apartment five weeks ago, although he'd called her numerous times, ordering her to return to him. That wasn't happening if Mitch could help it. He'd called a few contacts in the BDSM community and found a local, private club where she could be paired with a Dom willing to sign a no-sex contract with her until she was ready to move on. At least she would have the support she needed to resist her ex's advances. He'd quietly arranged a year's membership for her, paying for it out of his pocket. While he knew part of him was doing it for a submissive, who needed a break—which had sent his Dom protective instincts roaring—another part had done it because she was Tori's cousin, and Tori cared a great deal for her.

While Tiffany was his date, Mitch still couldn't keep his gaze from shifting toward Tori. He'd seen her in various outfits, consisting of club wear, lingerie, or street clothes, but this was the first time he'd seen her in a formal dress. The sleeveless, knee-length cocktail dress complimented her hourglass figure. The black, form-fitting top had a high, scooped neck, while the chiffon skirt alternated between black and bone-colored pleats. Mitch knew it was chiffon because he'd been listening to a few of Tori's female cousins gushing over the pretty dress. Otherwise, all he knew was she rocked it with the sexy, black, four-inch heels she had strapped to her feet.

Between the dress, heels, and her shouts of ecstasy echoing in his head from when he'd almost walked in on Tori and Ty last night and again around 2:00 a.m. from their bedroom, he was close to drooling. His gaze flitted to Ty, who was whispering something in Tori's ear, making her smile. Dressed in a custom black suit, white shirt, and red silk tie, the man complemented his woman. They were a good-looking couple, and once again, Mitch wondered what it would be like to be a third in a scene with them.

"Who the hell is this?"

Turning, Mitch noticed a red-faced man glaring daggers at him while clenching his fists. So, this was Tiffany's ex, Bruce Whitlow. Definitely not what Mitch had been expecting. The five-foot-ten Whitlow was at least fifteen years older than Tiffany, balding, and possessed that air of self-importance Mitch hated to see in Doms—or anyone else, for that matter. It was clear the bastard expected Tiffany to be quivering at his feet, even though they were in a non-lifestyle setting.

Mitch put his arm around Tiffany's waist and

tucked her into his side. He felt the trembling panic in her body and knew if he hadn't been there, she would have either fled or dropped to her knees.

Straightening to his full height, he gave Whitlow a death stare. "Name's Mitch Sawyer. And you are?"

"None of your fucking business," the man hissed. "And I wasn't talking to you—I was talking to my sub."

Oh, he didn't just announce to anyone in earshot that Tiffany's a submissive, did he? It was an unwritten rule in the lifestyle not to out anybody in public—community members valued their privacy. Thankfully, none of the other guests seemed to zero in on the reference. Mitch tugged Tiffany back a few steps and handed her off to Tyler before closing the distance between himself and the man he was dying to drop-kick across the room. Suddenly, the asshole didn't look so confident, and the color drained from his face. As Mitch suspected, the man was a coward who only bullied those who couldn't or wouldn't stand up to him.

Dropping his voice so only Whitlow could hear, Mitch growled. "I know exactly who you are, asshole, and you're not her Dom. Your contract is null and void. She's *my* sub now, and if you want to speak to her, you'll have to go through me. I want nothing more than to beat the living shit out of you right now, but I don't want to ruin things for the bride and groom. But if you so much as say one word to *my* sub without my permission, I'll be inclined to change my mind. Lose her phone number too. If I find out you're still harassing her, I'll make you dig the hole before I bury you. Understood?" Mitch almost chuckled to himself. Damn, he could channel Ian when he wanted to.

While Whitlow gaped at him, Mitch returned to Tiffany and pulled her to his side again. "Come, beautiful. Let's go to where there isn't a foul stench."

Leading his little group to another bar station, Mitch threw ten dollars into a tip jar as the bartender took their orders, then leaned down toward his date. "Are you okay, little one?"

Her accelerated breathing reverted to normal, but she was still pale, starkly contrasting her dark-brown hair and strapless, navy-blue, floor-length dress. Swallowing hard, she nodded. "Y-yes, Sir. I—I'm sorry."

Cupping her chin, he tilted her head until their gazes met. Her soft, chestnut eyes, so similar to Tori's, widened, and he almost regretted there was no spark between them. She really was a pretty woman. "There's nothing to be sorry about. You're safe with me, and that's all that matters tonight. Understood?"

She nodded. "Yes, Sir."

He placed a chaste kiss on her cheek. "It's Mitch, not Sir, while we're here. But as your temporary Dom, I'm ordering you to smile and enjoy yourself. Otherwise, I'll think I'm losing my charm." The corners of her mouth ticked upward at his teasing, and her smile widened when he winked at her. "Good girl. Now, let's have some fun."

As the cocktail hour turned into the dinner reception, Tiffany relaxed more and more, finally seeming to enjoy herself. There were still moments when she noticed her ex moving around the room and stiffened, but the man wisely stayed far away from the foursome. Mitch would let the Dom he'd investigated know that a mere verbal threat would probably keep the asshole away from Tiffany. The man was a police lieutenant in Vegas who'd helped several submissives recover from bad lifestyle relationships over the years, so it wouldn't take much to intimidate Whitlow. Mitch hadn't broached the subject of the whole setup with the sub yet but would talk to her tomorrow about it. She was taking him, Tori, and Tyler sightseeing for the day.

After dinner, the band picked up the beat, and everyone hit the dance floor. Mitch was glad he'd dated a woman in college who'd taught him how to dance because he had fun twirling Tiffany around. She and Tori traded partners a few times, but Mitch didn't have a problem with it until the band played a slower song while the woman he craved was in his arms. Her warm gaze was on him as he pulled her closer, unable to help himself. She placed her hands on his shoulders and followed his lead.

Shit. He shouldn't be enjoying this as much as he was. He couldn't even blame it on alcohol because he'd nursed the two glasses of whiskey he'd allowed himself since he was driving later. After getting into Tiffany's tiny Nissan Sentra last night, Mitch asked the hotel's elite client concierge to rent him a luxury SUV for the weekend. Mitch, Tori, and Tyler would drop Tiffany off at her condo on the way back to their hotel later.

With every sway of her delectable hips, Tori inched closer until their torsos brushed against each other. Mitch tried to recall every team who'd won the World Series to prevent his cock from responding, but it didn't work. He glanced over to where Ty was dancing with Tiffany and was surprised to see the other man nod at him. Either Ty had more to drink than Mitch thought he had, or he was saying that it was okay for the other Dom to top his woman. Had he noticed Mitch had been lusting after Tori? As co-owners of The Covenant, Mitch, Ian, and Devon did their best to know as many subs' hard limits as possible, although it was difficult with almost 200 subs. Copies of the lists were kept in files in Mitch's office and at the front desk for Doms to peruse. It helped when trying to steer the subs in the right direction to Doms who would be a good match for them. Okay, so maybe Mitch had studied Tori's limit list a little longer than most... and more than a few times. He knew a ménage was one of her green limits, which meant she'd experienced it at least once before and would be open to trying it again.

Not being able to resist, Mitch tightened his hold on Tori's waist and pulled her flush against him. A small gasp escaped her when she felt the erection his suit jacket was hiding from the rest of the party. Her eyes heated into pools of hot chocolate. Mitch tilted his head toward Ty, and Tori turned to see her Dom give another subtle nod, this time, aimed at her. A look of uncertainty crossed her face, and Mitch's heart sank. She wasn't receptive to the idea, and he'd respect that. Grabbing her hand from his shoulder, he spun her in time to the music, back into her lover's arms.

When Tiffany returned to him, Mitch kissed the back of her hand. "You look like you could use something to drink."

Her face was flushed from the activity, and he was glad to see she was having a good time. She smiled at him while trying to catch her breath. "I would love something to drink. This is the last time I wear velvet somewhere I'll be dancing up a storm. At least my shoes are comfortable."

He gave her his arm and gestured toward the bar. He'd noticed she'd switched from wine to soda after dinner. "One ice water for me and a Diet Coke for you coming right up."

Pushing Tori from his mind, he focused on caring for his temporary submissive. *Damn.*

"What was all that about?" Tori was sure she'd misread Mitch's interest up until the point she felt his hard-on. And she definitely hadn't misinterpreted Ty encouraging the other man, even though they'd discussed Mitch last night.

Her Dom shrugged as he danced her around the floor. "He wants you."

"And you want him. But he's straight, Ty. You're just setting yourself up for disappointment."

Leaning forward, he kissed her neck, which was exposed because her hair was in a fancy updo. She shivered as warm jolts of electricity shot through her, and moisture pooled between her legs. The same sensations she'd felt while pressed against Mitch's impressive erection.

"I'm just trying to take care of my submissive, baby. I'll move heaven and earth to give to you whatever you want."

Tori nuzzled her cheek against his. "You're all I want, Sir."

"Tsk-tsk. Lying to your Dom just earned you a spanking later, pet."

Shit. She should never have told him she was attracted to Mitch. If they had a threesome with him, she knew Ty would emerge from it more frustrated than ever because he couldn't have the man he was lusting over. Tori decided when they got back to Tampa, she'd suggest they start searching for a third willing to top the both of them regularly, so her Dom got what he needed as much as she did.

As the remainder of the reception progressed, though, Tori couldn't ignore the heat and want she saw in Mitch's eyes. It made her wish she'd taken Ty up on his offer of inviting the man into their bed as a third for a scene.

After they dropped Tiffany off at her condo, Tori worried her bottom lip as Mitch drove them back to their hotel. She was torn between her lover and her obsession. Yes, she'd been eyeballing Mitch for a while now, but she would never cheat on Tyler. However, that was no longer a problem with her Dom's permission. Could she handle both men at once? Could Ty come through the ménage unscathed?

With her mind spinning round and round, Tori didn't realize they'd pulled up to the Mirage until a valet swung open her door. Before she could climb out, Ty was there, extending his hand for her to take. When she stood, he tucked her into his side and whispered in her ear, "It's all right, sweetheart. Either way, whether you say yes or no is fine with me." As Mitch rounded the hood of the vehicle, Ty raised his voice. "Now that we don't have to worry about you driving, what do you say we hit the blackjack tables for a bit and throw back a few whiskeys?"

Mitch nodded as he shed his suit jacket and tie. "Sounds good. I'm sending this upstairs through the concierge if you want to get out of the monkey suit."

Grinning, Tyler pulled at the knot at his neck that he'd loosened earlier. "Awesome. I wouldn't mind so much if I didn't wear one at work most of the time. Thank God for casual Fridays."

When they reached the High Stakes Blackjack section of the casino, Tori thought she'd hit the nearby Joker Poker slots again, but Ty steered her toward a seat at an empty table between him and Mitch. "Join us, baby. Maybe you'll be our lucky charm tonight."

"*Um*... I really don't know how to play. I mean, I know the basics, but I'm always worried I'll piss another player off by doing the wrong thing."

Mitch threw a wad of cash on the table as he eyed the dealer's nameplate. "I think we can take care of that. Franklin, we'll take the whole table."

Reaching for the stack of bills, the dealer nodded. "Yes, sir."

There was room for six players, which meant each would be playing two spots—at $100 each. *Holy shit.* She couldn't afford that. Shaking her head, Tori tried to stand. "You guys play. I'll go to the slots."

"Sit back down, sweetheart." Tyler pointed to her chair. "This won't cost you a dime, but it's yours to keep if you win. I'll put up your money."

Mitch settled into his seat and signaled for a waitress. "If she's our lucky charm tonight, I'll pony up too.

And don't worry—I promise we'll help you and not yell, okay?"

Lowering herself back into her chair, Tori was still nervous. "Can't I just watch?"

"Uh-uh. The best way to learn is when you've got nothing to lose—and in this case, technically, you don't. Just be grateful we're not playing strip blackjack."

She giggled. "Is that like strip poker?"

"Yup," Mitch replied with a wink. "But it goes a lot faster."

Tori crossed her legs and put her small purse between her back and the chair. As the dealer counted out—*holy shit!*—$3000 dollars in chips for Mitch, Tyler placed his hand on Tori's knee and squeezed before subtly pushing the hem of her skirt a little higher on her thigh. Her eyes widened at him, but he only winked in return. He then pushed his own $2500 in cash toward the dealer. When the waitress approached them, Mitch checked with his companions, then ordered two whiskeys and a pinot grigio. Tori recognized the brands from when she'd bartended to get through college. If the drinks hadn't been free, they would've had to fork over a pretty penny for them.

The dealer began to shuffle the cards, and in the meantime, Mitch and Ty went over the rules and suggested play for specific cards. The waitress returned with their drinks as the dealer started tossing the cards in front of each bet. The first two rounds were no-brainers for her, and she won both, but on the third round, she drew a pair of eights on one hand and an ace and deuce on the other against the dealer's up card, which was a six. "Okay, so what do I do?"

Mitch pointed to the pair. "On that, you're going to double your bet and split them."

When she did as instructed, the dealer turned over a ten and queen, giving her eighteen on both. Then Tyler indicated the second hand. "You're doubling your bet on that, too, but you'll only get one card."

"Okay... I'm trusting you two." Tori crossed her fingers, but the dealer threw down a three. "Ugh. That sucks."

"It's not over until someone says their safeword," Mitch teased with a grin as he played his two hands.

Tyler roared as Tori chuckled and shook her head. "I can't believe you just said that!"

Mitch shrugged in amusement while watching to see what the new card would be on one of his hands, which he'd also double-downed on, before signaling he was staying on the other. When the dealer's hole card was turned over, it was a ten. With the next card thrown, the house busted with a queen, and Tori squealed and clapped. "Oh, my God! I just won $400!"

She grabbed the front of Ty's shirt, pulled him forward, and kissed him on the lips. "Thanks, babe!"

Without realizing what she was doing, she turned to Mitch and did the same. They both froze when her mouth crashed into his, but then his hand went to her neck, and his lips parted, sucking her upper one between his. Slowly, he pulled away as if savoring her taste. When he let her go, her gaze fell to the table, and she straightened in her chair. Embarrassed, she hoped the dealer didn't catch the sexual energy flying about the table between her and the men on either side of her. If they were in a BDSM club, it wouldn't have bothered her, but out in public, her old Catholic morals rose to the surface.

Ty squeezed her knee again, this time reassuringly, but he didn't miss the opportunity to push her skirt higher. Mitch definitely noticed and licked his lips before his gaze roamed upward. Ty kissed her bare shoulder. "You did good, sweetheart." He tossed a $25 chip toward the dealer. "Looks like we're going to have a lucky night, so let's share the wealth."

Tori's gaze went from Ty's to Mitch's. The heat she saw in both men's eyes had her squirming in her seat. Her clit began to throb with need, and her nipples tightened. How the hell would she say no if Mitch agreed to join them tonight if Ty asked him? A ménage was on her green list, and even if it was one of her soft limits, her Dom could still push her boundaries. Mitch would double-check to see if she wanted to refuse and use her safeword, but in her heart, she knew she wouldn't be able to.

Heaven help me.

CHAPTER FIVE

Laughing hard at something funny Mitch had just said, the threesome stumbled out of the elevator into their suite. Ty grabbed Tori around the waist to keep her from toppling over in her high heels. They'd had a great time at the blackjack tables, each winning. On the way to cash in their chips, the men had to keep shushing Tori because she'd announced to everyone she passed that she had won $2200. She was so adorable when she was a little tipsy. As always, she'd nursed her glasses of wine and drank water in between, but she was starting to feel the effects of what she'd imbibed. On the other hand, Ty stopped drinking the whiskey and switched to water after they'd gotten the first round of drinks at the table. He exchanged his almost full glass of the rich amber liquor for a bottle of water, knowing he would need his wits about him later to play if Mitch agreed to join them.

Wrapping her hands around his neck, she kissed him, and he was only too happy to kiss her back. Mitch brushed past them, and Ty wrenched his mouth from Tori's. "Mitch." When the man looked back over his shoulder, Ty spun Tori around, pulling her flush against his torso. "My subbie needs to thank you properly for helping her win all that money tonight."

As Ty gathered the material of Tori's dress in his hands, sliding the hem up her legs, Mitch's eyes flared with desire. Despite the few drinks the man had downed, there was no hiding the erection growing in his dress pants. Alcohol hadn't slowed him down one bit.

Mitch's gaze flashed from Tori to Ty's face. "You sure?"

"Wouldn't have said anything if I wasn't."

The man looked at Tori again. He stepped closer and gently cupped her cheek. "What about you, little subbie? Do you want me as a third with you and your Master tonight?"

Despite Tori's hesitation, her breathing and heart rate increased. Ty knew if he put his hand between her legs, he'd find her wet and needy. He whispered in her ear, "The decision is all yours, pet. But look how much he wants you. Let us both please you tonight."

She sucked in a shuddering breath. "Y-yes, Sir… Sirs. I want Master Mitch to join us tonight."

Leaning down, Mitch captured her mouth with his. Holding her head in place, he took what he wanted and, damn, if that didn't make Ty harder than the granite tiles they were standing on. Mitch eased up and kissed Tori on the tip of her nose. "Thank you, little one." His gaze darted to Ty's. "Lead the way."

"Hmm. Well, my little subbie earned a spanking earlier. We'll start with that after she changes into the sexy, red outfit she brought to drive me crazy."

Mitch grinned. "I can only imagine. Did you bring any toys?"

"Sure did." He gently pushed Tori toward their bedroom. "You have three minutes, sweetheart. Every second past that earns you more smacks." Making a show of setting his watch, he started the timer. "Better hurry."

The men chuckled as Tori's eyes widened before she ripped off her high heels and ran for the bedroom. Mitch then turned toward his own room, unbuttoning his dress shirt as he went. "I'll be back in a minute."

All Ty could only nod at the man's back and try not to drool. Damn, this was going to be the hardest scene Ty ever did. He was crazy for going through with it, but all that mattered was pleasuring his sub. If she was happy, then he was too.

Yeah, right. Keep telling yourself that, asshole, and maybe you'll believe it.

When Mitch returned moments later wearing nothing but a pair of jeans he'd had on earlier, Ty thought he'd gotten his desire under control. But the man's sculpted chest made his mouth water, and he lowered his gaze to the floor without hesitation. Damn, his submissiveness was rearing its head whether he wanted it to or not. Wishing he could have a little liquid courage, but knowing he couldn't have any more alcohol until after they scened, he strode toward the kitchen where they'd stored a case of bottled water.

He raised his voice so Mitch could hear him in the other room. "Want water?"

The urge to follow the question with a Sir had been strong, and he'd bit his tongue to keep it in as he eyed the other man through the doorway.

"Sure," Mitch responded while flopping down on the couch.

Ty nodded. Just as he handed the other man a cold bottle, Tori returned, and his jaw almost hit the floor. He knew what she'd brought in her suitcase, but this was the first time he'd seen it on her—and damn, she looked delicious. Her gorgeous, dark-blonde hair was back down from its updo, caressing her shoulders. Black lace boy shorts and a red and black bustier, with garter straps attached to the fishnet thigh highs peeking out from her over-the-knee black boots.

Glancing down at Mitch, Ty saw the same lust he was feeling written on the man's face. Shoving aside his desire to be topped, Ty stepped toward his woman and checked his watch. "Good girl. Right on time." He ran a hand down the side of her curves to her hip. "You look beautiful, baby, as always. Go kneel in front of Master Mitch while I change and grab a few toys."

Tori's breasts swelled with the deep breath she took, almost spilling out of their snug restraints. "Yes, Sir."

Hurrying into the bedroom, Ty shed his dress clothes and shoes and, like Mitch, grabbed the jeans he'd had on earlier. Pulling them up over his hips, he zipped them but left the top button undone. They'd be coming back off in a little bit anyway. His travel-sized toy bag was right where he'd left it on a chair, and he rummaged through it, selecting a multi-strand flogger, which he knew Mitch enjoyed using on subs, a little bullet vibe, condoms, and some lube.

Returning to the living room, he found Tori resting her head on Mitch's knee and the man stroking her hair while he sipped his water. Mitch lifted his gaze. "Ready?"

"Yup." He strode over to the window and pulled open the curtain so the lights of Vegas lit up the room. "Come here, little subbie. Time for your punishment before we have some fun."

Gracefully, Tori stood and, with her eyes downcast, walked to where he stood and waited for his next command. By the way she licked her lips, he knew she anticipated the scene more than dreading her punishment for lying to him earlier.

"Hands against the window, spread your legs, and

arch your back so that luscious ass is front and center for us."

As she followed his instructions, Mitch stood and joined them. Ty handed him the flogger, then took the bullet vibe, turned it on, and pushed the crotch of Tori's boy shorts aside so he could insert it into her core. As he'd suspected, she was soaked, and the little toy slid in without hesitation. Gasping, she clenched her muscles, and he stroked her legs. "Easy, baby. Relax. This isn't anything you haven't done before."

"Yes, Sir."

He straightened and moved to her side, then gestured to the leather implement Mitch was holding. "Her punishment is because she lied to me earlier when she denied wanting you as a third tonight, so it's only fair you dole out the punishment."

Mitch raised his eyebrow in surprise. Lifting the flogger, he ran it up the back of Tori's thigh. "Is that true, little one?"

The shiver that coursed through her sent goose bumps over her skin. "Y-yes, Sir."

"And why did you lie about that?"

She hesitated a moment before blurting, "I—I didn't want to hurt my Master by admitting I was attracted to you as much as I'm attracted to him, Sir."

Ty wasn't sure who was more shocked by her admission—Mitch or himself. Mitch's concerned gaze fell on Tyler's face. "Are you still sure about this? The last thing I want to do is put a rift between you two."

"I'm good," Ty stated with a nod. "I know she loves me, but if this is something she wants and needs, then I'm man enough to give it to her."

Mitch seemed to think about that momentarily, and Ty hoped the man wouldn't back out. Instead of stepping away, though, Mitch reached for Tori's chin and turned her head so she was looking at him. "I want to hear you say it again, little one. No misunderstandings, and I need to be sure it's not the alcohol talking, although I noticed you sipped yours more than I did mine, and Ty stopped altogether."

Tori's tongue darted out and wet her lips. "I'm sure. Please give me my punishment so we can enjoy a scene together, Sir."

A grin spread across Mitch's handsome face. "Since that was such a polite request, who am I to deny it?" He tossed the flogger on a nearby table. "But since alcohol is a factor for me this evening, I'll let your Master give you your punishment in the form of a spanking. I'm afraid I might hurt you more than intended."

Although Mitch was obviously feeling some effects of the whiskey, Ty was glad that at least one Dom in the room had his head on straight. It was a hard rule that no one was allowed to play in The Covenant if they consumed more than two drinks. Most of the members rarely exceeded more than one, and some none at all before play. Drinks were tallied on digital membership cards nightly, and checked on handheld computers by the staff before members were allowed to enter the play areas. "Good idea. I didn't think of that. Thanks."

"No problem. I also think my aim would have been off."

Well, maybe the man was a little drunker than Ty thought as he saw him sway a little on his feet. The men switched places, and Mitch sat on the window seat Tori was leaning over. The edges of her boy shorts were high enough to expose most of her cheeks. Ty squeezed one side of her ass and then the other, bringing the blood to the surface so she wouldn't bruise. Mitch cupped one of her breasts. "Ready, love?"

"Yes, Sir."

"Count out loud to twenty."

Before the words were completely out of Mitch's mouth, Ty reared back and slapped Tori's ass with his open palm. She squeaked and went up on her toes. "One, Sirs."

Ty vigorously rubbed her skin and then held the heat in with his hand a moment before spanking her other cheek.

"Two, Sirs."

Her breathy voice was torture for Ty's cock. As he continued to mete out her punishment, Mitch slid his body between Tori's and the window. Tugging the top of her bustier down, he exposed her breasts so he could play. His lips closed around one nipple while his fingers teased the other.

"Oh, God! Seven, Sirs."

Skimming his other hand down the front of her torso, Ty pushed the lace aside and found her clit already peeking out from its hood. As he rubbed it, he could feel the vibrator doing its job inside her. Tori's breathing hitched as she counted each slap, and knowing his lover's body well, he warned, "No coming until your punishment is done, pet. Otherwise, I'll give you another twenty on top of that."

"Twelve, Sirs! Yes, Sir!"

As Ty gave her a moment to catch her breath, Mitch let her tit pop from his mouth and leaned around her hip to eye her ass. "Damn, she reddens beautifully." He caressed her warm cheeks for a moment, then grabbed her boy shorts and pulled them higher on her hips. "Oh, yeah. Fucking gorgeous."

Lifting his head, Mitch leaned back and stared at Tori's face. Despite her tears, Ty knew what the other man saw in her eyes. Want. Need. Pain. Pleasure. Submission was what Tori craved. As a switch, Ty understood that more than most Doms.

When Ty started slapping her ass again, Mitch plucked her taut nipples, causing Tori to close her eyes and bite her lip, probably trying to control her urge to come. "Thirteen, Sirs! Fourteen, Sirs! Oh, God!"

Mitch smirked at Ty. He'd dropped one of his hands between Tori's legs, and his thumb strummed her clit. It was just enough to keep her on the edge of her orgasm, but the experienced Dom read her body's responses—her squirming, increased breathing, and keening—and halted his torture before she could fly. Of course, that made her beg. "Please! Oh, God! Fifteen! Please, Sirs! Hurry! Sixteen, Sirs!"

When she shouted, "Twenty," Mitch pushed hard on her clit with his thumb. "Come, baby."

Tori screamed her release, and Ty hoped the floor, walls, and ceiling were soundproofed. Otherwise, they might have a visit from security. Her body shook with the intensity of the orgasm, and he wrapped his arms around her waist to keep her upright. Mitch's fingers didn't let up, drawing out her pleasure as long as he could. "Damn, she's even more beautiful when she comes."

Tyler silently agreed as he nuzzled her neck and rubbed his erection against her red and sore ass. When her trembling eased and her body sagged against him, he leaned down and tucked his arm under her knees. Lifting, he carried her over to the "L" shaped couch while Mitch pushed a large plush ottoman closer to give them all room to relax. The extra piece converted the furniture into an extra-wide chaise lounge.

"Are you okay, baby?" Ty moved her hair back from where it had fallen across her face and studied her.

"Mmm-hmm. Can I take my boots off, Sir? They're usually comfortable, but my feet hurt from being in heels all day."

"Sure." As Mitch removed her boots, Ty reached behind her and found the tie to release her bustier. "As a matter of fact, let's get you completely naked and get that vibe out. We're not done with you yet."

It wasn't long before all three of them were naked, and Ty tried hard not to stare at Mitch. While not as muscular as his cousins, the man was still a fine specimen of the male anatomy—tight, lean, sinewy, and well-endowed. Ty clenched his ass, aching to have Mitch fuck him. *Damn*, he really needed to focus on Tori before he did something stupid.

With the men lying on either side of her, Tori wrapped her hands around their cocks, pumping slowly as they licked and kissed her face, ears, neck, shoulders, and everything else they could reach. Moans, heavy breathing, and wet noises filled the room. Ty lifted his head to watch the other two French kiss, but his gaze kept going to Mitch's crotch and his impressive erection. The purple head wept, and Ty wished he could lean forward and lick it.

Trying to get his mind off the other man, Ty turned his attention back to Tori. Nudging her hip, he instructed, "Straddle him, baby, so he can fuck you while I take this fine ass."

When she was in position, Ty handed her a condom to put on Mitch. While he was sure Tori was clean and protected, he hadn't asked Mitch about his medical history, which, as the club owner, was probably fine. At The Covenant, condoms were mandatory for all vaginal and anal sex, regardless of a couple's marital or long-term relationship status.

As Tori rolled the condom on Mitch, Ty squeezed some lube on his fingers, then ran them down the crack of her ass to her hole. Once she was ready to receive him, she went up on her knees and slid down on the other man's cock until he was buried to the hilt. Mitch's eyes fluttered shut as he gripped her hips and held her still. "Hurry, Ty. She's killing me here. So fucking hot and tight. Damn!"

Placing a hand on Tori's bare back, Ty pushed gently until she was draped across Mitch's torso. As the two of them kissed again, Mitch spread her ass cheeks for Ty. Lining up his cock, Ty eased into Tori's ass, a little at a time. She moaned as he gained access, and Mitch had to squeeze her hips tighter to keep her from squirming.

Finally, Ty was in as far as he could go without hurting her. Her ass was as hot and tight as her pussy, and he could feel Mitch through the thin membrane separating them. He involuntarily groaned at the thought and hoped it wouldn't be recognized for what it really was in response to. Gritting his teeth, he said, "Whenever you're ready."

"Thank God," Mitch responded as he began to withdraw and plunge back into Tori's wet heat. On his forward thrust, Ty did the reverse, pulling part of the way out before going deep again.

The two men were soon fucking her in sync, taking her higher and higher. Mitch sucked on one of her tits while Ty spanked her already red ass a few times. He felt her gasps and moans all the way to his toes, but it was the drag of Mitch's cock against his that had him speeding up his pace. He wished he could make it last longer for all of them, but the need to come was beyond anything he'd ever experienced.

Reaching around Tori, Ty slid his hand between her and Mitch, enjoying how his knuckles brushed against the man's hard flesh. His fingers found Tori's clit and began to tease and torture it.

Mitch's thrusts also picked up speed. "Shit! Let her come, man!"

As the other Dom bit down lightly on her nipple, Ty pinched her clit, and Tori screamed. Her vaginal walls rippled around the cock inside them, and Ty could feel it in her ass. A few more pumps and Mitch roared his release, with Ty following. He held himself deep as he came, and lights, as bright as the neon ones outside the window, flashed behind his closed eyelids. His lungs heaved for oxygen as Tori sagged on top of Mitch, who was also gulping for air.

When he was sure he could stand without falling, Ty pulled out of her ass, then placed a loving kiss on her lower spine. "Stay with Mitch, sweetheart, while I get a washcloth."

"Yes, Sir," she mumbled into the other Dom's chest, causing both men to chuckle.

A short time later, all three were curled together in a heap on the couch and ottoman, engaging in pillow talk. It had been hours since they ate at the wedding, and they placed a call to room service for several appetizers, a bottle of Pinot Grigio, and a bottle of Jack Daniel's Single Barrel Select. When there was a knock on the door, Ty threw on his pants to answer it. He signed for the food and drinks, then took the wheeled cart so the uniformed man wouldn't walk in and see Mitch and Tori still naked and relaxing on the couch.

While the others spread out the food, plates, and napkins, Mitch poured two whiskeys for him and Ty and a glass of wine for Tori. The TV was turned on, and they ate in the nude while watching *Young Frankenstein* on a classic movie channel. The three of them laughed at the antics of Gene Wilder, Marty Feldman, and the rest of the cast, and Ty couldn't get over how natural the whole thing felt. It was as if he, Tori, and Mitch belonged together. Or was that just wishful thinking?

Tori had fun feeding both men, which, of course, filled the room with sexual energy again. After another round of drinks, it didn't take long before the men began to kiss, lick, and explore the woman's luscious curves once more. With her back to Ty, Tori wrapped her hand around Mitch's cock as it grew hard. Ty ran his hand up her hip and torso, over her shoulder, and down her arm while kissing and nipping her back.

Mitch moaned and thrust his erection into Tori's hand. "Harder, pet."

Nuzzling Tori's neck with his beard, Ty threw caution to the wind, closed his hand over Tori's, and squeezed. "Like this, baby. Like you're almost going to break it off."

Palming Tori's breast, Mitch chuckled, seemingly oblivious to the fact that he had another man's hand around his cock, even though a woman's hand was in between. His words were a little slurred as he spoke. "Just don't actually try to break it off—I'll never recover, and there'll be a lot of disappointed subbies out there."

Ty pumped Tori's hand up and down, then hesitated when she removed it and plunged it into Mitch's hair. The other man's hips thrust forward, and Ty couldn't help himself. Tightening his grip again, he started the same up-and-down motion he'd been doing moments earlier, but there was nothing between his palm and the velvety, hard flesh this time. Mitch was too tipsy and busy making out with Tori to realize what was going on, and Ty kept telling himself he should let go before he got punched, but he couldn't.

Leaning down, he licked Tori's hip, which was so close to what he really wanted to lick. Suddenly, he felt Mitch freeze, and a hand grabbed Ty's hair—hard.

Fuck! I'm so dead.

Letting go of the man's cock, Ty dared a glance up at him and opened his mouth to apologize before a brawl started. But what he saw in Mitch's eyes wasn't anger. Instead, there was confusion and, holy hell, lust. Without conscious thought, Ty licked his lips.

He could feel Tori's body tense between them as she realized what'd happened—no one said anything. Seconds ticked by as a war raged in Mitch's eyes.

"Let us please you, Sir," Tori whispered as she bravely placed small kisses along Mitch's jaw. She must have sensed he was seriously considering letting Ty continue. The Dom's gaze went from the switch to her and back again. "Just us. No one has to know."

Suddenly, there was a tug on Ty's hair, and it took him a moment to realize the Dom was pulling him toward his cock. He should say no and back off. Mitch was drunk and would regret it in the morning. He really should laugh it off like it was a big mistake—which it was—but instead, he let himself be led. His gaze met Mitch's once more, and the man gave him a slight nod.

Maybe Ty had been wrong. Maybe Mitch had played with other men in the past. Right or wrong, Ty parted his lips and took a tentative swipe at the pearly liquid oozing from the purple head. His gaze never left Mitch's, and the desire he saw there flared. Opening his mouth, Ty wrapped his lips around the cock and moaned. The sensations caused Mitch to flex his hips, and Ty took him to the back of his mouth and swallowed.

"Fuck!" At the man's muttered curse, Ty tried to lift his head and let go, but the hand in his hair pushed him back down. "Don't fucking stop."

As Ty began to blow him in earnest, Mitch turned

his attention back to Tori's breasts, but his hand stayed on the back of Ty's head, occasionally flexing and pulling the short hair to the point of pain.

Bringing his hand up between Tori's legs, Ty found her wet and ready for him. He eased two fingers into her core and began to fuck her. The three of them became a mass of squirming, moaning, and gasping flesh.

He didn't know how much time passed as he licked and sucked Mitch and finger-fucked Tori, but Ty didn't care. He could do it for hours. Without warning, Mitch pulled his hips away, and Ty worried he'd had a change of heart. But that look of lust and need was still on the man's face.

The Dom in Mitch took over as he rolled to his feet and began to search the couch and floor. His voice was low and commanding. "Tori, on your knees—Ty, fuck her."

Ty and Tori exchanged a look as Mitch found what he was looking for—the bottle of lube. *Holy shit.* Maybe they'd both underestimated Mitch. Maybe he was a closeted bisexual.

When Tori got on her hands and knees, Ty positioned himself behind her and lined his cock up with her slit. Cool liquid drizzled between his ass cheeks.

Oh, God, he's really going to fuck me!

As Ty eased his erection into Tori's heat, one then two fingers breached his ass and began to stretch him, lighting up the nerves in his rectum. It made him even harder as he dragged his cock in and out of Tori's tight pussy. After a few torturous minutes, the fingers slid from his body, and then he felt something much larger at the entrance to his hole.

Mitch pushed his cock past Ty's sphincter and groaned loudly. "Fuck! So fucking tight! Damn!"

Mitch fucked Ty as Ty fucked Tori, and the middleman was in fucking heaven. Mitch's cock stretched him, and with each thrust, Ty wanted to beg for more. The combination of having his dick surrounded by Tori's tight walls while Mitch's was in his ass was pure ecstasy. It wasn't long before he felt a tingling down his spine, straight to his balls. One of Mitch's hands released Ty's hip and, without warning, slapped his ass cheek.

Ty couldn't stay quiet. "*Ah*, shit! Again, Sir! Please, again!"

This time, his other cheek felt the sting. "Damn right, again," Mitch growled as he alternated spanking both sides of Ty's ass. "Topping from the fucking bottom."

Underneath him, Tori keened as her breathing and moaning accelerated. "Oh, please! I can't hold back! Please let me come!"

"Sir, please let us come." While Ty would normally top her, he was a sub in the ménage this time, so he deferred to the Dom.

Mitch thrust his hips a few more times before answering. "Come! Both of you!"

That was all the encouragement Tori needed as she cried out. Her pussy quivered around Ty, and moments later, he followed her into an orgasmic abyss. "FFFFuuuuuccckkkkk!"

"Good subbies. Such a tight fucking ass. Does that feel good, sub? I'm going to come in this ass, and you're going to fucking take it."

Ty's chest heaved. "T-Tori, lie flat."

He slid out of her when she followed his command, then put his hands on both sides of her shoulders, supporting his upper body and bracing himself. "Please, Sir. Let me have it. You feel so fucking good."

Grabbing hold of Ty's hips again, Mitch's hard flesh slapped against Ty's ass and thighs as he sped up. "Take it, subbie. Take fucking all of it."

"Yes, Sir!"

Bellowing a string of curse words, Mitch plunged deep and froze as streams of cum filled Ty's ass. It took a moment for the latter to realize what was different. *Shit! No fucking condom! Damn, Mitch better be clean.*

When the Dom's cursing stopped, and he'd caught his breath, he pulled out and rolled onto his side on the oversized ottoman. As his eyes fluttered closed, he muttered, "Damn, that was fucking hot."

Within minutes, Mitch and Tori were sound asleep, and Ty was left wondering what the fuck had just happened and if it would ever happen again.

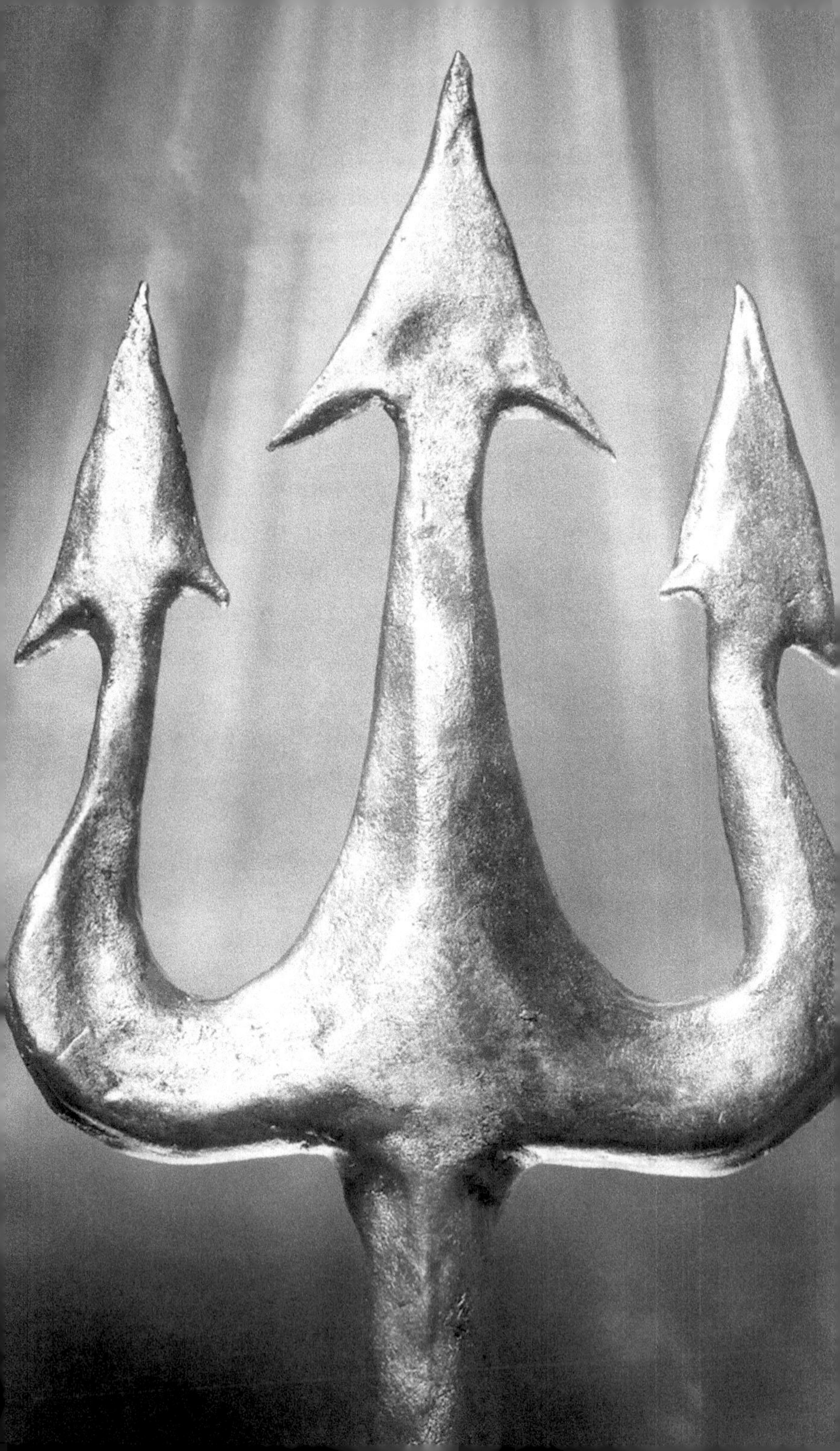

CHAPTER SIX

Blinking, Mitch rolled over in his bed and glanced at the clock on the nightstand. 6:15 a.m. His head hurt like hell, and his tongue felt like it was covered in cashmere. He was also naked as the day he was born with a healthy case of morning wood.

Shaking the cobwebs from his brain, he froze. *What the...* Flashes of the scene he'd shared with Tori and Ty appeared in his mind. *Holy shit! I... we... Ty had... Holy fucking shit!*

Feelings of shock, revulsion, and lust waged a battle within him. Running a trembling hand down his face, he swung his legs to the floor and sat up. The memories of what he'd done swirled in his mind like a tornado, and the pounding behind his temples didn't help. It was a dream... it had to be a dream... didn't it? *Shit.*

His bladder screamed to be emptied, and he stood

and stumbled to the bathroom. Flushing the toilet, he turned to the sink and washed his hands, then cupped some water and splashed it on his face. He studied his reflection in the mirror. His bloodshot eyes and tousled hair were a sad addition to the coarse stubble covering his jaw and upper lip.

Jesus H. Christ. He'd fucked Tyler in the ass last night *and* gotten a blow job from him to boot. *What the fuck?* Mitch had never been attracted to a man in his life. So, what the hell had he done last night and why?

Anger coursed through him, and he started for the bedroom door but pulled himself up short. He couldn't beat the shit out of Ty—it wasn't the other man's fault. Yeah, Mitch remembered how it started but also how he didn't stop it and even encouraged Ty to continue. It wasn't like he'd been raped—he'd wanted it at the time. Hell, he'd topped both Tori and Ty during the scene. He'd enjoyed what they'd all done.

So why are you freaking out now? Because the urge to bust into their bedroom and have a repeat of last night is strong, and you have no fucking idea why. Shit!

No! I'm not gay... not even fucking bi-sexual! I've never wanted to have sex with a man before, so what the fuck changed? It had to have been the alcohol, right? Fuck!

Alcohol might have been a factor, but he'd still been in control. He'd known not to flog Tori because he could have hurt her. He could've told Ty to back off, but what did he do? He'd grabbed the man's hair and encouraged him to suck his cock. Then he'd flipped positions, and as Ty fucked Tori, he'd fucked Ty. And, *shit! Without a fucking condom!*

The unwanted visions of the scene sprung to his mind again and... *fuck!* His morning wood was coming back with a vengeance. Mitch ran his hands through his hair, gripping the strands, almost pulling them out of his head. He had to get out of there before they woke up. He couldn't face them right now... hell, he wasn't sure he could face either of them ever again.

Stumbling back into the bathroom, he turned on the shower and didn't bother waiting for it to warm up. A cold one was what he needed right now until he could sort things out in his mind. Minutes later, he was dry, dressed, and packing his things. After a quick glance around to ensure he hadn't forgotten anything, he listened at his closed bedroom door for any signs Ty or Tori were up. Hearing nothing, he slowly opened the door and found the common area empty and their bedroom door shut. Spotting the rented SUV's keys on a table in the foyer, he left them for Ty and Tori. He trusted them to return it to the rental company tomorrow— he'd put the other man down as a second driver on the agreement. Mitch could grab one of the cabs, which were undoubtedly queued up by the valet.

As the elevator dinged its arrival, Mitch heard a toilet flush. *Fuck!* When the doors opened, he hopped into the car and hit the lobby button more times than necessary until the doors shut again. The elevator began its descent, and Mitch sighed in relief, but it only lasted a moment or two.

What the hell am I doing?

He couldn't just go back to Tampa, hide in his condo or office, and forget last night had happened. The moment he saw Ty and Tori again at The Covenant, he was sure to have a deer-in-the-head-lights look on his face, and then everyone would know what they'd done. *What happens in Vegas, stays in Vegas? Yeah, right.*

A plan formed in his mind, and by the time the elevator reached the lobby, he knew where he was going and who he would talk to when he got there. But first, he had one other thing to take care of.

When the cab pulled into the condo complex and idled at the curb, Mitch got out, leaving his bags in the trunk. The driver had agreed to wait for him, thanks to the promise of a generous tip. Mitch didn't know how long he'd be, but had told the man it would be about fifteen or twenty minutes.

Striding to the unit he'd escorted Tiffany to both nights he'd taken her home, he rang the doorbell. Glancing at his watch, he winced and hoped he wasn't waking her up at such an early hour, but he wanted to speak to her before he left Vegas. This time, he lifted his hand to knock, but the door swung open.

Mitch narrowed his eyes at Tiffany, who was dressed in a long robe and had a curious expression on her face. "You opened the door before asking who it was, little one?"

Her gaze dropped to the floor. "Sorry, Sir. But I looked through the peephole and saw it was you."

Relaxing his shoulders, Mitch tried to put her at ease. His mood wasn't the result of anything she'd done or said, and she didn't deserve to feel apprehensive around him. "I'm sorry, Tiffany—I just want to make sure you're safe. Do you mind if I come in for a few minutes? Something's come up, and I'm heading to the airport after this. I apologize for missing your sightseeing tour."

She opened the door wider and let him in. "That's okay. I understand. I'm glad you stopped by, though, because I really want to thank you for all you did this weekend. I couldn't have gotten through the wedding without you, Sir."

"You're welcome. It was my pleasure." Following her into the understated living room, he sat in the recliner she gestured to and saw her hesitate before sitting on the couch, her eyes downcast. He knew she'd almost gone down on her knees at his feet. "Tiffany, look at me." When her gaze met his, he continued. "This is a conversation between friends, not Dom/submissive, or slave for that matter. I want honest answers from you, but beyond that, you don't need to follow protocol. You don't need to call me Sir unless I indicate otherwise. Okay?"

The younger woman took a deep breath and let it out slowly. "Okay, Si... I mean, Mitch."

"Good girl." He pulled a piece of paper out of the back pocket of his jeans and handed it to her. "I asked around through my club connections and found a Dom who's willing to take you on as a contracted sub without sexual relations. Cordell Roberts is a police lieutenant with the Vegas PD and a well-respected Dom in the lifestyle. I had him completely vetted, even though he's a cop. He's currently without a sub and has helped several subs get past bad D/s relationships. I've arranged a year's membership for you at the club he belongs to. Are you familiar with Club Domain?"

Wide-eyed, she nodded. "Y-yes... but I can't afford—"

Holding up a hand, he cut her off. "Like I said, it's been taken care of—you have a full year there. All you need to do is call Master Cordell. His number's on that paper, and he's expecting your call. If you don't feel comfortable with him, let me know, and I'll find someone else. My number is under his." He shook his head and grimaced. "Whitlow really screwed with your head, sweetheart. He's everything most Doms hate. He wanted a slave... not just a D/s slave, but the type that was abolished over a century ago, no matter the race. And I don't think a Dominant/slave relationship is what's best for you, but that's for you to decide, which is why I want you to speak to Master Cordell. He'll help you understand your needs from a different perspective and how to have those needs met. You're a beautiful woman, Tiffany, and I'm not only talking about your physical features. You're beautiful, here..." He pointed to his forehead and then his heart. "... and here. I think Master Cordell will be able to make you realize that, and that you deserve the very best from any Dom who's lucky enough to catch your eye next.

"Master Cordell will also encourage you to speak up and say your safeword if you need to, and more importantly, he'll respect that safeword. Everything will stop, and you'll openly discuss what went wrong without repercussions and how to prevent it from happening again. Saying your safeword should never result in any punishment—whether it's physical, emotional, or mental." He paused and let that sink in for a moment. "You were afraid to use your safeword with Whitlow, weren't you?"

Her embarrassed gaze fell to her lap. "Yes, Sir... Mitch."

Standing, Mitch stood and went down on his knees in front of her, taking her hands in his. She flinched, clearly surprised to see him in a submissive position. "Tiffany, you should never feel afraid in any relationship you have—D/s or not. That's not what the lifestyle's about. Feeling anxious and on edge is normal, but being afraid is not. Understand?" He squeezed her hands, trying to reassure her things would be all right.

She nodded. "Yes, I think I do. Why... why did you do all this? For Tori?"

"No—I did this for you. One of the things I love most about the lifestyle is taking care of submissives in whatever way they need. It was an honor to be your Dom this weekend to ensure your safety and well-being. You're a sweet woman, Tiffany, and you deserve the best Dom you can find. Promise me you'll call Master Cordell and negotiate a no-sex contract with him, or call me if it doesn't work out, and I'll find someone else."

A smile spread across her face. "I promise. Thank you, Master—I mean, Mitch. Sorry, it'll take me a while to break the habit. This is the nicest thing anyone has ever done for me."

Getting to his feet again, he leaned down and kissed her cheek. "Your future is going to be filled with nice things, sweetheart. I have to get going. After you speak to Master Cordell, call me and let me know how it went, okay?"

"Okay. I hope he's as nice as you. I'm sorry you can't join us today." She stood and followed him to the door. "Next time you're in Vegas, let me know, and I'll give you the non-touristy tour."

"You're on. Goodbye, little one."

Three hours later, Mitch was settled into a First-Class seat on a plane bound for San Diego. He'd gotten hold of his cousin, Nick Sawyer, and his fiancé/Dom, Jake Donovan, on the way to the airport to make sure they'd be around when he arrived. Nick had been surprised and a little concerned about the impromptu trip, but Mitch had assured him all was well. At least, he hoped he'd assured him because, as far as Mitch was concerned, things were far from well. He had no problem with anyone who was gay or bisexual—he had numerous friends who were. That was one thing about the BDSM community—there was no right or wrong way to be attracted to someone or play. Being open-minded was almost a requirement. There was such a wide variety of kinks, and more were popping up every year as people experimented with different ideas.

The problem Mitch was facing was he'd never been attracted to another man in his thirty-four years on Earth, so why was it happening now with this man... with this couple? Wait. Was that it? Was it because it was Ty *and* Tori? He knew several members of his club were involved in permanent ménage relationships—some with two males, others with two females. Among them, a few participated in full ménages where one Dom or Domme topped both sexes.

"Sir, would you like something to drink?"

Mitch gave the flight attendant a slight smile he didn't really feel. "A bloody Mary, please."

Maybe a little hair of the dog would get rid of the

last of the pounding in his head the Advil he'd swallowed earlier hadn't touched. He settled further into the luxury seat. In less than an hour, he'd land in San Diego and Nick would be waiting for him at the airport. But Nick wasn't the person he wanted advice from. Jake was. Mitch prayed the other Dom would help him figure out what the hell was going on. If not, things were sure to go to shit when he returned to Tampa.

Shaking her head, Tori walked back into the bedroom, where Ty was still under the covers but awake. "He's gone," she said.

Rolling onto his back, Ty's eyebrows shot up. "What do you mean, 'he's gone'?"

"Just what I said—he packed up and left. No note, no nothing."

Flinging the covers off his naked body, her lover marched out to the common area and into Mitch's bedroom to see for himself. Probably not because he thought she was kidding him, but more to see if she'd missed something, which she hadn't. Pulling the hotel robe tighter around her body to ward off the chill she was feeling, Tori sat down on the bed and waited for Ty to accept that Mitch had run after last night's encounter. While she'd loved every minute of it, she should have expected that Mitch wouldn't be happy about it this morning when he woke up and remembered what'd happened.

The man had staggered back to his own bedroom to use the bathroom, and a few minutes later, when she checked on him, he was sound asleep. She'd pulled the covers over him and gently kissed his lips before closing the door on her way out. Whatever had gone through his mind this morning, it was probably better he'd woken up alone.

Tyler returned and sat on the bed beside her, dropping his head in his hands. "I fucked up. Big time. He's going to fucking kill me."

"If he were going to kill you, he'd have done it before he left. He's confused… and probably scared." *Hmm.* That was a word she never thought she'd associate with either Mitch *or* Tyler. But last night had pushed the former out of his comfort zone, and the latter was regretting the fact he might have ruined a friendship and any chance of Mitch ever talking to him again. Tori's heart clenched. The Dom would probably avoid her as well in the future, and that hurt more than she'd expected it to.

Last night, when everything had fallen into place, and the three of them had scened together, uninhibited, it had felt right to her—like she and Ty had found the person who made them complete. Most people only needed one person to make them whole, but she and Ty were different. And now she doubted they'd ever find their missing piece again because he'd walked out the door and out of their lives.

"Maybe he just needed some space, and everything will be fine when we get home tomorrow." Tori tried to sound optimistic, but her words rang hollow even to her own ears. "But there's nothing we can do about it now, so let's get dressed and have breakfast. I saw Mitch left us the keys to the rental. We'll get Tiffany and go sightseeing like we planned."

Ty stood and started yanking clothes out of his suitcase. "Maybe I should call him and apologize."

Raising an eyebrow, Tori shook her head. "No. Give him space. We'll call him when we get home." Stepping over to him, she ran her hands up his bare arms. "Please... Sir. Let's enjoy the day."

Sighing, he pulled her into his arms and kissed her. "What did I ever do to deserve you, pet? You're the best thing that's ever happened to me."

"Ditto, Sir."

CHAPTER SEVEN

M itch had no trouble spotting his dark-haired, blue-eyed younger cousin outside the airport security gate. Nick was the one a half dozen teenage girls and several older women were drooling over. Dressed in snug faded jeans and a blue Henley, his handsome baby face, combined with the muscular physique the Navy SEALs had given him, tended to be a draw for both sexes, no matter where he went. Unfortunately for the ladies, Nick was gay and madly in love with his fiancé.

When Nick spotted Mitch, a huge grin spread across his face. A firm handshake was accompanied by some back-slapping. "Hey, cuz! Decided to visit the Golden State before heading back home, huh? It's good to see you."

"Same here. Thanks for picking me up. I had to

check my bags, so we need to hit the baggage claim." He looked up and checked the signs, but Nick was already headed in the right direction. "So, excited you're going to be an uncle again?"

"Yup. Unlike when JD was born, I'll be there when Angie pops this little rug rat out. I'll miss California, but I'm looking forward to joining Trident, working with my brothers, and being closer to the family. It's time."

Nick had about four more months before his last tour of duty was up, and he'd already let SEAL Team Three know this was his last one. Mitch couldn't imagine how hard a decision that'd been for him, as he often spoke of his teammates being his brothers as well. But with Jake by his side, it was time to move on and start a more stable life together. They'd both be taking assignments with Trident, but hopefully, those wouldn't be as dangerous as the ones they'd faced in the past under Uncle Sam. Although, the company did have contracts with the government, so Mitch could only speculate.

"Has Jake picked someone to head the West Coast team when you're ready to head east?"

Stepping on an escalator going down, Nick nodded. "Almost. He's narrowed it down to two people and will have a powwow with Ian and Dev about it next week. I think they'll wait to make the final decision until after they dump both teams in the

Rockies for their final training runs. The Omega team will be doing that in a couple of weeks. Then they'll schedule TS West for the same drill."

Mitch had heard all about that. Ian and Dev wanted to ensure the teams could work together as cohesive units. They'd be airlifted by helicopter to a remote section of the Rocky Mountains, where they'd be set down with minimal gear. It would be at least a two-day hike out of the wilderness. A satellite radio was only to be used in extreme emergencies, and from what Mitch understood, a broken bone didn't qualify —only life-threatening injuries did. As usual, he was glad he'd gone the college route and gotten his MBA.

While they waited for his bags, the conversation turned to the Dom who'd been brought in for questioning about the serial killings yesterday. Nick widened his stance and crossed his arms, which made his biceps bulge. "Jake and I talked to Dev last night. Like you, we couldn't believe it. I mean, I've only met the guy once or twice, so you all know him better than I do. Hell, there are over four hundred people in that club now—I'm lucky I know a dozen or so names to begin with. But like I said, you know him. Is he capable of this?"

Eyeing the suitcases coming around the carousel, Mitch shook his head. "I'd like to think he's not, but then again, I never thought anyone could be capable of torturing those women to death with a bullwhip. I mean, how well do we ever really know anybody? You hear it all over the news every day when people are arrested for doing the unimaginable—their family and friends always say they never saw it coming."

"True."

Mitch spotted his bags and squeezed between a toddler with his mother and an older gentleman to grab them before returning to Nick. "Let's get out of here. I don't know about you, but a beer and some greasy food sound awesome right now."

Grinning, his cousin led the way to the parking garage. "When am I not in the mood for beer and food? I'll call Jake from the car and tell him to meet us."

Twenty-five minutes later, they walked into a pub on Coronado Island that was popular with people from the nearby Navy base—especially the SEALs. At twelve-thirty, the place was in full swing with the lunch crowd, and there wasn't a table available. Nick added his name to the hostess's on-call seating list while Mitch snatched up two stools at the bar, which had just been vacated. His headache was gone thanks to the bloody Mary and two bottles of water, but that didn't stop him from ordering two Bud Lights for him and Nick. Jake would be there in about ten minutes, and Mitch was even more nervous about the conversation he needed to have with the other man. At least he knew Jake would be the very last person on Earth to judge him.

Glancing around, Mitch found his gaze landing on

several men. Deep in his gut, he felt... nothing. The place was filled with good-looking, physically fit men and women, yet he couldn't say he was attracted to any of them. He sure as hell couldn't picture himself having sex with one of the men in the establishment, so why did his cock twitch every time he thought of Ty and Tori? And when had the two become one in his mind? It was almost like one of those Hollywood couples who the media combined their names to be cute, like "Bennifer." He couldn't think of one without the other. So, did that make them "Torty" or "Tyri"? Jeez, he was fucking losing it if he was searching for a cute name for the two of them. Mitch didn't do *cute*. At least, he never had before.

Joining him at the bar, Nick waved at a few men playing darts in a side room and asked one of them to put his name on a chalkboard for the next game. He sat next to Mitch and took a swig of his beer. "Those are a few guys from Team Five," he explained before turning the subject around again. "So... want to tell me what this visit is really about?"

Mitch's eyes narrowed. "What are you talking about? One of the club's submissives asked me to join her and her Dom at a wedding in Vegas. Her cousin just got out of a bad D/s relationship, and the guy was going to be there. I figured I'd stop in for a visit since it was only an hour's flight here. I don't have to be back at the club until Wednesday."

Any hope he had his cousin bought the half-story

was dashed when he arched an eyebrow at him. Mitch scoffed. "Dude, face it. It's probably a good thing you're a sub because you'll never get the Dom stare right. Although, you have the deadly SEAL glare down pat, so that makes up for it."

The corners of Nick's mouth ticked upward as he chuckled. "Yeah, well, as long as I've got deadly down, I'm good. But there are definitely times I'd love to throw that Dom stare at Jake and make it work."

A hand slapped Nick's shoulder, causing him to startle and turn, only to find his fiancé towering over him with a frown and narrowed eyes. "You mean this Dom stare, Junior?"

A loud, exasperated sigh escaped the younger man. "Yeah, that one. But I can't be in trouble for wishful thinking, right?"

Jake smirked. "Oh, you can be in trouble for anything I come up with."

"Hey, Sawyer, you're up!" One of the men at the dart board gestured him over.

Standing, Nick gave Jake his seat. "Saved by the fucking bell. Listen for my name to be called for a table."

As his submissive strode away, Jake grinned and shook Mitch's hand, then ordered a beer before taking Nick's seat. "Good to see you. What brings you to the West Coast on such short notice? Not that I mind. You just usually make plans weeks in advance."

"The opportunity popped up, and I took it." When

Jake gave him the same look Nick had given him a few minutes ago, Mitch knew the man wasn't buying the weak excuse. However, where Nick's was lacking in intensity, Jake's wasn't—he knew something was bothering him, but he'd wait until Mitch was ready to talk.

"Nick! Party of three!"

Thankfully, the hostess's announcement gave Mitch a few more moments to figure out how to broach the subject of what had happened in Vegas. They took their beers and followed her to a table in the rear of the pub after catching Nick's eye to let him know where they were headed. Knowing Jake preferred to keep his back to the wall in any establishment, like all the other men at Trident, Mitch took the chair facing away from the center of the room. The hostess dropped three menus on the table and said their waitress would be with them in a few minutes before leaving.

Jake eyed Mitch curiously. "So, what's on your mind?"

His gaze pinned to the beer bottle in his hand, Mitch took a deep breath then exhaled slowly. This had been a lot easier in his mind. "How did... shit... how did you know you were gay?"

The other man's brows shot up almost to his hairline. "What? Um... okay, not anywhere close to what I thought you were going to ask, but I'm sure there's a point to it."

"Yeah, but can you answer that before I get into everything?"

Jake shrugged. "All right. I figured it out when I was in my early teens. While all the guys were checking out the girls' asses, I was checking out the guys'. At first, I fought it—even lost my virginity to a girl in high school—but after that, I finally admitted to myself that I was gay." He paused. "I've seen you screw a lot of women, Mitch, so if you're telling me you're switching teams, then I'll assume you're bi. Tell me what's going on. Obviously, something happened, and now you're confused."

Mitch snorted. "That's a fucking understatement. I don't even know where to start."

"How about at the beginning?"

Jake sipped his beer and waited patiently. It was one of the reasons Mitch had sought the man out. In addition to being gay and not one to judge, Jake was what some people might call an "old soul." He was easy to talk to and could help people analyze their feelings instead of brushing things off. However, it had taken the guy falling for Nick to finally deal with his own demons.

Leaning back, Mitch ran a hand through his hair. "Do you remember Parker's friend, Tori? She's the one who trains the dogs for veterans with PTSD."

"She hooked Russell up with a dog after he got out of the hospital, right? Yeah, I think Boomer told me she joined the club."

"Yeah. Well, I've had a thing for her, but with everything going on lately, the new wing, the homicides, and other stuff, I waited too long to approach her. Tyler Ellis collared her about two months ago."

Jake nodded. "Tyler's a good guy. He'll treat her right."

Mitch hadn't expected Jake to say anything more about the guy, even though he'd scened numerous times with Ty when the switch had wanted to be dominated. That'd all stopped when Jake and Nick became a couple. A jealous pang coursed through Mitch at the thought of Jake and Ty together, which confused him even more. "I know that. That's not the problem. Tori asked me to go to Vegas with them this weekend. Her cousin's a sub who just went through a bad breakup with her asshole Dom and needed an escort because the guy was going to be at the wedding they were all attending. I said yes. Part of me agreed because of Tori, the other part was I really didn't want to be at the barbecue back home. It seems like everyone is either engaged, honeymooning, or pregnant. It was kind of getting to me."

"Understandable. It does seem like we've had a population explosion in the extended family." When Mitch remained quiet, Jake prompted, "Okay, so you went to Vegas with Tori and Ty... and what happened?"

His mouth twisted in annoyance. "You're going to make me say what you've already figured out."

"That's step one in figuring out what's going on in that head of yours, so, yeah, I'm going to make you say it."

He let out a long and heavy sigh, then glanced around to see if anyone was listening to their conversation. Leaning forward, he lowered his voice. "A ménage got out of hand—I had a few more drinks than I usually do and had sex with both of them. And I've never been so fucking confused in all my life."

"Why should you be any different from the rest of the world?" The snark had Mitch glaring at Jake, who chuckled. "Okay, okay, I'll ease up. Did you talk to Tori and Ty this morning or sneak out and run?" Mitch didn't respond as his gaze dropped to the table. "Okay, you ran. Again, understandable. So, my next question is, do you want it to happen again?"

There was the million-dollar question, and God help him, he didn't know the answer. "Fuck, I don't know. Did I enjoy it at the time? Yeah. But what the fuck? I've never been attracted to men before, so why now? And in my head, the two of them have become one. I can't see myself with one without the other."

Jake rested his arms on the table and leaned forward. "So, option one is top Tori, but tell Ty sex with him is not going to happen again. But, as you just said, you don't want one without the other—and they may not go for that either. Option two—walk away from both of them. Option number three—see where this goes. You're not the first guy—or woman, for that matter—who suddenly found themselves attracted to a member of the same sex. Sometimes, it just takes the right person for those feelings to surface." He paused. "Are you afraid of your feelings, or how everyone will react when they find out? Most of your friends will be cool with it, being in the lifestyle and all, but what about your family? I know Ian, Dev, and Nick won't have a problem. Neither will your aunt and uncle. But what about your folks and brother."

Shrugging, Mitch picked at the beer bottle label. "It's not like they don't know I own a lifestyle club. And between Nick and two of my cousins who are gay on my mom's side of the family, everyone's fine with that too. So, I guess the answer to your question is, yeah, I'm afraid of these feelings I'm having. It's like the first thirty-four years of my life have been a lie."

"I wouldn't say a lie. It's more like you were biding your time until the right person came along—or, rather, the right couple. You've been involved in ménages before—does this feel like there's more to it than just scening with them?"

"You're asking if I want a relationship with them where I'm topping them both?" Jake nodded. "I don't know—I really don't. Part of me wants to run for the hills, while the other part is screaming at me to get back on the fucking plane and go find them."

"Nick's headed this way, and I'll understand if you want to keep this between us for now. But I'll tell you what—feel free to crash in the spare bedroom for a few nights while you get your head straight. I've got work stuff to deal with tomorrow, but Nick's got a week off before some new training starts. It'll give you some time to relax and think."

"Thanks. That's an option I can deal with right now."

Ty was nervous as hell. They'd been home for two full days without hearing from Mitch. He and Tori had left a few messages on the Dom's cell and office phone at the club, with no return calls. It made Ty realize that, although he'd known the man for over four years, he had no idea where Mitch lived or how to get in touch with him outside of The Covenant. But tonight, they'd see him at the club—or, at least, they hoped so. Wednesday nights were usually slower than the rest of the week, but plenty of members would still be stopping in for a few hours to play.

Reaching over from the passenger seat of Ty's BMW, Tori squeezed his rigid forearm as his hand gripped the steering wheel harder than necessary. He glanced over and saw understanding in her eyes. "It'll be okay, Sir. Whether he blows us off or not, we still have each other."

His heart sank. He was sure Tori was convinced Mitch wouldn't want anything more to do with them, and that hurt. Could he return to being friends—or more like casual acquaintances—with the man? Ty didn't think so. It would probably be best if he and Tori found another club to join. There were a few other private clubs in the area—he refused to go to a public one because the rules tended to be lax, and there was no vetting process. He didn't want to leave The Covenant—he really liked the people there and everything else about it. But if things were going to be uncomfortable—miserable was probably a better word—then it was best they resign their membership.

Ty took Tori's hand and brought it to his lips, his gaze still on the road. "As long as I have you, pet, I'm good. But I almost wish Vegas had never happened. I'd rather have Mitch topping you than not topping either of us." His gaze flashed to hers for a moment. "I know you could have fallen for him."

Tori looked at him in alarm. "I'd never leave you!"

"*Shh*, pet. I know. But that doesn't mean you don't have feelings for Mitch too. I saw it in your eyes in Vegas, and I can see how disappointed you are that he probably doesn't want anything to do with us after what happened."

Getting off the highway at the exit for the compound that housed both The Covenant and Trident Security, Ty pulled up to the new gatehouse. A few months ago, the media had gone crazy after learning that Grayson and Remington Mann were club members, along with their new submissive, Abigail. The Mann brothers owned Black Diamond Records, a well-known production company. A vengeful ex-lover, who'd also been one of their top recording artists, had ratted them out to the media, and the shit-storm that followed resulted in upgrading the security at the compound. From what Ty had heard, however, was that the woman who'd instigated everything had gotten her ass kicked—figuratively. The Mann and Sawyer brothers had gotten their revenge, which had cost the singer dearly.

The fence line and guardhouse had been extended about a quarter of a mile, and more guards and some K9s had been added to keep the media and lookie-loos out. One positive thing from it all was the increase in membership requests. With the opening of the new wing, the Sawyers had raised the maximum number of members from 350 to 500. Each new Dom or submissive, though, was utterly vetted through Trident Security before being accepted. The BDSM community valued their privacy, and the process to clear people was very thorough.

Ty rolled down his window and handed the guard his and Tori's club cards, which were scanned into a hand-held device. This was another added layer of security. The guards would be alerted if any member had been suspended or expelled. The cards were also used to keep track of alcohol consumption, bar billing, and medical clearances.

A flash of panic coursed through Ty. What if Mitch had suspended their memberships? He was one of the owners, so, technically, he could suspend or expel anyone for any reason he saw fit. But to Ty's relief, the guard gave him back the cards and waved him through the gate. Finding a parking spot, he was back to feeling anxious when he spotted Mitch's car. At least they knew he was here tonight.

While Tori headed to the women's locker room to change into her fet-wear, Ty scanned the people scattered throughout the bar area, down in the pit, and in the garden, without finding the man he was looking for. The door to the office was shut, but he could see a thin line of light on the floor. Raising his hand, he took a deep breath, and pushed the doorbell used when the music in the club was pounding, then waited. In addition to the chime, a red light would turn on over the door inside the room, just like at a newsroom or radio station to indicate they were "on the air."

When there was no immediate answer, he was about to walk away. Then he heard Mitch rumble, "Come in."

Ty hesitated a few seconds, then turned the knob and pushed the door open. Mitch was sitting behind his desk, and from the deer-in-the-headlights look, he hadn't been expecting Ty to be his visitor. Sometime in the past few days, he'd shaved his face clean, which made the man even more handsome.

This is all or nothing, Ty thought to himself. *Do it for Tori.* Shutting the door, he purposely dropped his gaze to the floor, went down on his knees—shoulder-width apart—and clasped his hands behind his lower back—just like a good submissive would. "Permission to speak, Sir."

There was a long silence, and he fought the urge to lift his gaze to see the other man's expression. Was he going to kick him out or let him say his piece?

"You may get up and sit in a chair, Ty."

Holy shit, that was Mitch's Dom voice. He recognized it immediately, and an involuntary shiver of anticipation went up his spine. Swallowing hard, Ty stood, took one of the guest chairs, and waited.

"Look at me." When Ty raised his chin and their gazes met, he saw turmoil in the man's eyes but not anger. He held tight to a fine thread of relief as Mitch continued. "First of all, don't stare at me like you're afraid I'm going to fly over this desk and beat the shit out of you. I don't blame you for what happened the other night—you may have instigated it, but I was a willing participant." He paused. "As you've probably already figured out, I freaked out the next morning."

"I'm sorry if I embarrassed you, Sir."

A snort escaped Mitch. "Embarrassed is not the word I'd use. Hell, I'm not sure what word I'd use." He leaned forward and ran a hand through his hair. "Ty,

I've never... ever... had sex with another man before, much less been attracted to one. All that changed the other night, and I'm still dealing with how I feel about it."

Ty felt a glimmer of hope. "May I ask how you *are* feeling about it, Sir?"

Glancing away, the Dom inhaled a deep breath, then let it out again before returning his gaze to Ty's face. "Where's Tori?"

The change of topics caught him off guard. "She's... um... in the women's lounge, changing."

Mitch nodded. "Good. Get her, and see if playroom sixteen is available. If it's not, find one that is and let one of the DMs know where you'll be waiting for me." Ty's jaw dropped, and his eyes widened, but Mitch kept talking. "All three of us will talk when I get there. You have ten minutes... and I expect both of you to be on your knees."

Holy shit! "Um... y-yes, Sir." Ty stood and hurried out of the room before the other man changed his mind.

He didn't say you were going to play, asshole, so keep it together. Don't get psyched up about something that probably won't happen. Maybe he just wants to explain to both of you at the same time that nothing else is going to happen. Or maybe he just wants to top Tori. But why wouldn't he just talk to us in his office? Why the playroom?

Ty racked his brains, trying to remember what was in Playroom 16. It was one of the dozen new themed rooms that had been added on with the new wing. There were twenty-four of them now, and he hadn't played in all of the new ones yet. Would he be crossing off another room on his to-do list? Only one way to find out.

Mitch stared at his office door—the one Tyler had shut on his way out—and wondered what the hell he'd just done. He'd spent the past few days in San Diego mulling over his options and how he felt about everything. When he'd gotten home to Tampa this afternoon, he'd been no closer to having an answer. He should've known he was out of time—Tori and Ty were often at the club on Wednesdays. So why was he here? It wasn't like the staff couldn't function without him for one night, and he could've had an extra day to figure out what he wanted to do. But as soon as Ty had stepped through the door, all thoughts of why it might not be a good idea to get involved with him and Tori had fled Mitch's mind.

The man was wearing black leather pants, a vest, and boots. Combine them with his handsome face and excellent physique, and Mitch's cock had twitched. But what had made him hard, almost to the point of pain, was when Ty had dropped to his knees in a perfect submissive position and asked for permission to speak. It had taken everything in Mitch not to order the man to strip so he could fuck him. But something had been missing. Actually, *someone* had been missing —Tori.

Damn, he had it bad. Maybe another scene or two and his desire to top Ty would go away. And perhaps it wouldn't. *Shit.*

Standing, he adjusted himself in his own brown leathers. At least, no one would be the wiser if he joined the couple in a playroom. He'd been a third in scenes before, so anyone paying attention wouldn't think he was doing anything more. And as sure as he was that the sun would rise tomorrow, he knew there would be *more* in that room tonight. He was going to top both of them—and with a completely sober mind tonight.

The doorbell buzzed, and the red light above the door lit up again. Mitch froze for a moment. Was it Ty coming back to say he'd changed his mind? No, it was highly unlikely. Mitch had seen the lust in the other man's eyes before he left to find Tori. There was no way Ty would back out of a scene tonight.

Taking a seat at his desk again, he bellowed to be heard over the music out in the hall, "Come in!"

The door swung open, and Master Stefan Lundquist strode in. The tall Coast Guard lieutenant had been a club member for over a year after being promoted and transferred from a base in New Jersey. He was currently in a month-long contract with

Cassandra, one of the club's waitresses. "Hey, Mitch. I brought in that catalog so you can order the nice jute rope I use."

Master Stefan was an expert in Shibari, the Japanese art of rope tying popular in the BDSM community. He'd given a demonstration recently, and several Doms had expressed interest in taking a class he'd volunteered to teach, which was scheduled to begin next month. Mitch had wanted to stock the type of rope Stefan preferred in the club store for them to purchase easily. This particular jute was specifically made for Shibari in Japan, and the only wholesalers were located there.

The man handed him a thin catalog with only about ten pages. "You'll want to place an order this week to have it in time for the class."

"Thanks. I will. Two more Doms signed up. Do you want to limit the class size?"

Lundquist shrugged. "It's best to keep it under ten so I can give more one-on-one attention. Too many and not everyone will get the most out of it. I can always run another class."

A thought came to Mitch's mind. "You'd be willing to do more than one?"

"Sure. It lets me practice and experiment more. How many do you need?"

"I've been talking to a few other private club owners, and we were thinking about offering cross-training—their members would come here and vice versa to attend classes on nights the clubs are closed. If you can do three four-week classes throughout the year, I'll discount your membership fee for your time."

The man thought about it for a moment, rubbing a hand over his salt-and-pepper crew cut. "I think I could manage that, but six classes are better for each group. Since you're closed on Mondays and Tuesdays, I can do them here for three weeks. Is that all right with you?"

"Perfect. I'll cap the participants at ten and tell the others they can sign up for the next one. I'll contact the other owners and set up a rotating schedule they can post and add to. Is Cassandra going to be your sub for the class?"

"Yeah, at least for this one. I'll have to renegotiate at the end of our contract. Why?"

"Let her know I'll pay her for her classroom time." He knew the pretty waitress had already volunteered to do it for free, but it was only fair to reimburse her for being tied up during the demonstrations on her days off.

Stefan nodded. "Sounds good. Oh, and for the jute, plan on ordering the twenty-five footers, with a couple of thirty-foot lengths just to have handy. Each Dom will need at least one hundred feet of rope for the class, and they'll learn to adjust what they need from that. I circled the ones I prefer in the catalog with the suggested diameters for you, but almost anything from that company is top of the line."

"Great. I'll place the order tomorrow and make sure they have it here at least a week before the class starts. After that, I'll keep plenty in stock at the store." Mitch stood and glanced at the clock. He was already two minutes late and needed to get downstairs. "I've got to head down to the rooms."

Exiting the office, Stefan went to the left, out toward the bar area, while Mitch headed right to the new stairs that would take him to one of the hallways that housed the playrooms.

At the bottom of the steps, Master Cain Foster was on DM duty. Foster was one of the two leaders of the Trident Security Omega Team. Since he could get deployed on a mission at any time, he tried to get all his shifts in as early in the month as possible so no one would have to cover for him. With his arms crossed over his muscular chest, the former Secret Service agent nodded at Mitch. "Ty said to tell you they're in room sixteen."

"Thanks."

As suspected, the man didn't seem to think it was odd that Mitch was joining the couple in a scene, and that was how he preferred it. He didn't want anyone to know what was happening behind closed doors. *Shit.* He stopped outside the door to the playroom and called himself almost a dozen names equivalent to the word "coward." *Damn it.*

Could he do this without Ty thinking there was more to it? And what about Tori? Could Mitch continue to scene with her without falling in love with her? Because, *damn it*, he was already halfway there. This whole mess reeked of disaster, yet he couldn't stop himself from wanting both of them more than he wanted his next breath. Call him selfish, but he'd deal with the fallout later—and there would definitely be some type of fallout after this was all over.

Kneeling, her eyes downcast, with Ty at her side, Tori held her breath as the door to the playroom opened. The theme for this particular room was the "Principal's Office." The usual cabinets along the wall next to the door had been replaced with high school lockers to store play implements and supplies. A beautiful mahogany desk with an executive chair sat on one side of the room, while on the other were a couple of side-by-side spanking benches. Two St. Andrew's crosses were against the fourth wall. The rest of the decor was similar to what one would expect in a college dean's office. Hard-covered books filled a few shelves on a bookcase by the desk. The "school colors" of red and gold were used throughout, and there were also items from schools and college fraternities like cheerleading pompoms, a wooden spanking paddle, rulers, and numerous other items that could be used in some sort of play.

When Ty had found her, she'd been shocked Mitch wanted them to meet him in a playroom. Out of all the scenarios of how this evening might turn out flying around her head, this hadn't been one of them. She only hoped whatever the club owner had in mind, Ty wouldn't be disappointed. She'd been serious with her Dom earlier—if Mitch only wanted her, then there would be no negotiations between them.

She wanted to look up to see Mitch's expression, to hopefully get a glimpse of what he was about to say, but she didn't want to start whatever this was with a punishment. So, she waited... and prayed.

For a few moments, she heard nothing but her and Ty's breathing. Anxiety caused her heart rate to speed up. Finally, the sound of footsteps reached her ears, and suddenly, Mitch's brown leather boots entered her range of vision and stopped in front of her—well, not exactly in front of her, but in front of both of them.

A sharp, inhaled breath came from beside her, but neither she nor Ty said a word.

Mitch's voice rumbled with the authority of a Dom. "Subbies, I'd like to negotiate a scene with you. Are you willing?"

"What would the scene entail, Sir?" Ty asked, the hopefulness in his tone unmistakable.

"Look up—both of you."

Tori raised her chin, and her mouth watered at the

sight of Master Mitch. In addition to his leather pants and boots, he wore a white dress shirt with the sleeves rolled up to his elbows. The first few buttons were undone, and a smattering of dark chest hair peeked out. He had shaved since the wedding, and his jawline and upper lip looked soft and smooth. The beard had given him a bad-boy look she loved, but seeing him clean-shaven really got her juices flowing. His piercing blue eyes darted from Ty's face to hers and then back again.

"Although I said I didn't blame you for what happened the other night, you were topping from the bottom—both of you were, although Tori was a lot more subtle about it—and I won't allow that again. We'll start with a flogging for punishment to remind you of that fact." The Dom paused a moment, letting his words sink in. "After that, I'm interested in a ménage—a full ménage—on one condition—what happens in this room stays here. Same goes for Vegas. I'm not sure how I feel about all of this, but I do know I enjoyed the other night—enough that I want to see if it was just a one-time thing. I don't know if this will be the last time, so don't ask. I want your utmost discretion when we leave this room. Understood?"

Tori could keep his secret, but she wanted to hear Ty's response first. This affected him more than her. Mitch studied the other man's face. "Ty, answer me."

Out of the corner of her eye, she saw Ty nod slowly. "Yes, I can agree to that tonight, Sir."

What he hadn't said hung in the room. He wouldn't appreciate being someone's dirty little secret for long. At some point, Mitch would have to come clean or step out of their lives forever.

"Tori?" Mitch's blue eyes bore into her with a combination of lust and need.

"Yes, I agree, Sir."

"I do have one question, Sir," Ty added. When Mitch gave him a nod, he continued. "In Vegas, you didn't use a condom with me." Mitch winced at the reminder. "It'd be irresponsible if I didn't ask if your medical clearance is up-to-date?"

"Yes," the Dom responded, "three weeks ago, and it's on file at the front desk. It's a mistake I won't make again." All medical releases and limit lists were available for members to inspect to ensure everyone's safety. "Anything else?"

When both subs replied that there wasn't, Mitch took a deep breath and stepped back. "Stand and strip." Striding to the lockers, he opened one and selected a nine-tail leather flogger.

Tori watched him as she removed what little clothing she had on. It was ironic that Mitch had chosen the Principal's Office without seeing what she'd been wearing. She had chosen a school girl's plaid skirt with a white lace bra tonight.

Turning back to them, he waited until they were both naked before speaking again. "Tori, stand in front of the cross, facing it." He continued when she took the instructed position at the cross on the right. "Ty, fasten her ankle and wrist on that side."

Ty attached her left limbs while Mitch took care of her right. Once she was fully restrained, Mitch had Ty take the same stance in front of the second cross and quickly fastened the leather bands to his ankles and wrists. He then took a moment to double-check the circulation in both subs' feet and hands, running two fingers between the leather and their skin, ensuring the restraints weren't too tight.

"Safeword, subbies."

The couple responded in unison, "Red, Sir."

A shiver coursed up and down Tori's spine. She heard Mitch moving about the room but didn't dare turn her head to see what he was doing. Moments later, another locker door opened and then shut again. Her heart pounded, and she'd be surprised if she were the only one who heard it.

Without warning, the knotted tails of the flogger slapped across her ass and kept going over Ty's. The sting had her gasping, however, she knew from watching her Dom scene with other men, it was nowhere near how hard it needed to be for him. But then the sound of leather against flesh resounded again, and Ty hissed. "Shit!"

Mitch let out an almost evil chuckle. "If you thought I would go easy on you, Ty, think again. You get two for every one Tori gets because I know you can handle it."

"Yes, Sir."

Another swipe fell across Tori's ass, and she willed the pain away, trying to concentrate on the heat. She could say her safeword at any time, and she knew Mitch would heed it, but she also knew she and Ty needed this—craved the discipline as much as the pleasure that would follow—and she would take her punishment. Strike after strike, she got wetter and more turned on despite the fact this was a punishment and tears were rolling down her face. She knew without looking that Ty's cock would be almost unbearably hard, but he, too, took what was coming to him.

Her ass and thighs felt hot, and she could almost imagine how red they must be. Another strike landed, and she couldn't hold back the cry that escaped her. Mitch stopped and stepped forward, placing his hand gently over her abused flesh. "Give me a color, Tori. An honest one."

Her jaw trembled. "Y-yellow, Sir."

Reaching up, he released her wrists before bending down and undoing the restraints around her ankles. He picked her up in his arms and held her against his chest. At some point before they started, he'd removed his shirt, and she reveled in the warmth of his skin. Mitch glanced at Ty.

Her Dom's concern was palpable. "Damn it, Tori. Why didn't you say your safeword before this?"

"I—I was just about to—I was g-good until that last one."

Mitch scowled at her. "I can't read minds, pet, only body language. If you don't give me a verbal warning, I could hurt you badly, and that's the last thing I want to do." He raised an eyebrow at Ty. "Are you okay while I get some ointment on her?"

"Yes, Sir. I'm good and still green."

With a nod, Mitch carried Tori to a set of gym mats that were on the floor next to the spanking benches and gently laid her down on her stomach. He stood but quickly returned, and Tori hissed as he began to smooth the pain relief ointment over her tender skin. "There shouldn't be any bruising, sweetheart, but you'll be sore for a day or two."

"It's okay, Sir. That's already working. I'll be okay in a few minutes."

When he was done with her care, Mitch brushed her hair off her face and grinned. "Rest, and after I'm done with Ty, we'll have some fun, okay?"

She returned the smile. "I'm looking forward to it, Sir."

After placing a blanket over Tori's body to keep her from getting chilled, Mitch stood and strode back across the room to take care of his other submissive. His gaze dropped to Ty's ass which was bright red, with criss-crossed welts that would fade in a day or two, and yet the man wanted more. Mitch's hard cock twitched in his leathers, and he inwardly cursed his attraction. He released Ty's restraints and held his arm to stabilize him as he led the way back to where Tori lay. The woman appeared to have drifted into subspace as the pain in her ass had morphed into pleasure, but she was alert enough to move over and give Ty room to lay down beside her.

Mitch grabbed the ointment tube and began to apply it to the red areas on the other man's flesh. He couldn't help but notice the difference between Ty's muscular ass and Tori's softer, curvier one. Both were beautiful in their own way. Mitch had always been an "ass man," but never before had it been a man's ass he'd admired. Again, jolts of confusion flashed through him, and he tried to dismiss them from his mind. No one outside knew exactly what was happening in this room, and if the two subs kept their word, which he thought they would, no one would ever know.

Ty let out a low moan as Mitch rubbed the ointment into his muscles. "Are you okay, Ty?"

"Yes, Sir. Better than okay. Horny okay. Subspace okay. All's good."

A smile spread across Tori's face, and Mitch winked at her. "Glad to hear it."

He finished that part of the aftercare and

retrieved three bottles of water from a small fridge and handed one each to Tori and Ty. There was a full fridge in each theme room since play tended to dry people out. This way they didn't have to wait until they got ahold of a waitress or made their way up to the bar.

Downing his own water, he watched Ty turn on his side and kiss Tori before lifting his gaze to the Dom. He zeroed in on Mitch's erection, which couldn't be concealed if he tried, and licked his lips. "If Sir wishes to continue, I'm ready."

Mitch eyed Tori, who nodded. Tossing aside the empty plastic bottle, his hands went to his leathers, and, holy hell, as the two enjoyed the brief strip show, he grew even harder if that was possible. "On your knees."

After they followed his order, he stepped toward them and, with his thumb and index finger, tilted his cock until it was parallel to the floor. "Lick me. Together."

Both subs moved closer, and their tongues slid past their lips and met his hard flesh. Mitch groaned. "Again. Don't stop."

His breath hitched as their tongues dueled with each other and circled around his girth. It was the most erotic sight he'd ever seen, and that was saying a lot, considering the lifestyle he'd lived for over a decade. Cum pearled at the tip, and Ty swiped it before Tori could.

The switch looked upward. "Permission to use our hands, Sir?"

His the corners of his lips ticked upward. "Granted."

Ty reached up and cupped his balls, and Mitch's eyes shut, and his head fell back on his shoulders. *Fuck! I shouldn't be enjoying this. But I can't stop it. Feels too fucking good.*

Tori's movement had him opening his eyes again as she lowered her head and sucked one of his balls into her mouth. Mitch swayed on his feet and slapped his hand on the spanking bench next to him for support before he could fall on his ass from the sheer pleasure he was receiving.

Since Tori was now busy with his balls, Ty sucked Mitch's cock into his mouth and sealed his lips around it. His cheeks hollowed, and Mitch saw stars. "Fuck! Again!"

His free hand went to the back of Ty's head, gripped his hair, and set the pace he wanted. Tori's hands explored Mitch's legs, ass, hips, and torso, dragging her nails across his skin. It sent shivers up his spine. Hell, everything was sending shivers up his spine. His breathing accelerated. "Faster," he ordered with a growl.

The two subs increased their ministrations, and Mitch felt a pressure building in his scrotum. "Shit! Suck together!"

A lightheadedness began to overtake him, and like

a dam bursting, he came in Ty's mouth, and the switch swallowed every drop as Mitch's legs shook with the force of the orgasm. As a sense of peace came over him, he pulled from their mouths and dropped to his knees, gasping for air.

God help him. That was better than anything he'd dreamed of. And, damn it, Vegas hadn't been a drunken fluke. *Fuck!*

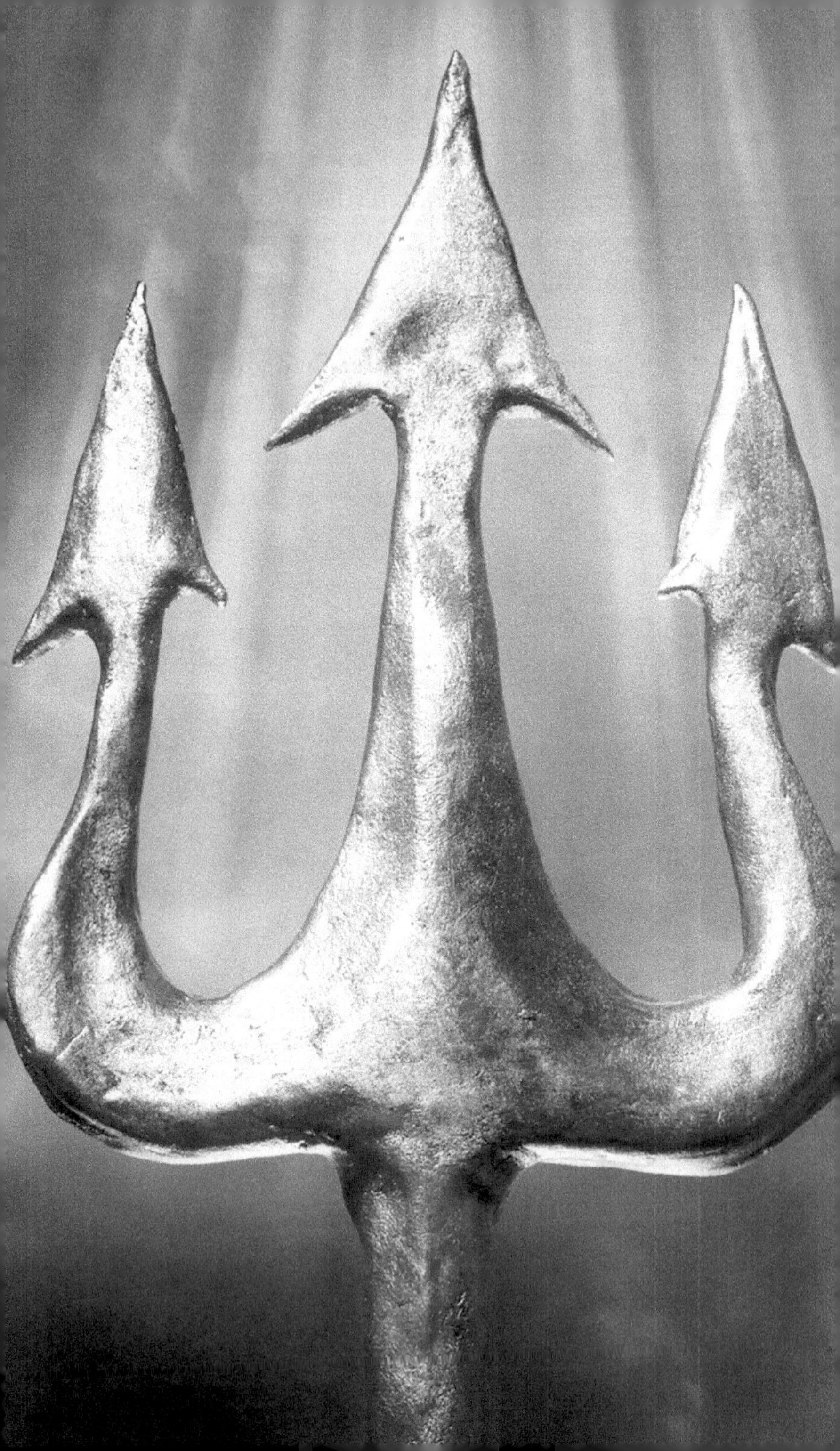

CHAPTER TEN

Pulling into the parking lot of Mitch's condo, Ty wondered what the man had wanted to talk to him about tonight. It'd been four weeks since that first night at the club, and since then, the three of them had scened together four to five times a week—sometimes at the club, other times at either Ty or Mitch's place. They'd even had a few evenings when they did other stuff, like going out to dinner or a movie or staying in and taking turns cooking dinner.

However, tonight was different. Mitch had called him and asked him to come over for some beer and pizza and to talk—without Tori. Ty highly doubted the Dom would include beer and pizza in a conversation, saying he'd changed his mind about the contract they had all signed a few weeks ago.

Ty had entered into the agreement, reluctantly,

due to a clause about keeping the details of the ménage from anyone else and now he was truly regretting it. He didn't want to be anyone's closet obsession, even if he'd fallen head over heels for the guy. Somewhere along the line, Ty's feelings for Mitch had become as strong as his feelings for Tori. He couldn't imagine going back to being just a twosome. If Mitch left them, Ty's heart would be ripped out of his chest, and he knew Tori felt the same way. The problem was that they didn't know how Mitch felt about them.

Another thing that was bothering Ty was that in all the scenes they'd done, not once had Mitch kissed him on the lips or cock. It was like all he was interested in was fucking Ty's ass or mouth. Any other man, Ty could have accepted that—at least if there was an end date on a contract. But with Mitch, he craved to have the Dom make love to him as he did Tori—with everything inside of him and no holding back. Ty wasn't sure how much more he could take before he ripped up the contract.

Climbing the few steps to the condo, he knocked and waited. The door swung open, and Mitch waved him in as he spoke into the cell phone he held to his ear. "Yeah, Ian, I'm still here. What's up?" There was a pause, and then Mitch paled before his expression became thunderous. "Are you fucking kidding me? How many more subs are going to be taken before they nail this fucking guy? Wait... what about—"

His words were cut off as Ty followed him into the living room and sat in one of the recliners. It was clear the serial killer had struck again and another submissive had gone missing. So far, none of the victims had been members of the Sawyers' club, but there could be numerous reasons why. Rumor had it that a Dom from The Covenant had been questioned by the FBI about the killings but was released because there hadn't been enough evidence to charge him. The name of the Dom had been kept quiet, and Ty assumed the feds had been watching him carefully. This new kidnapping probably cleared the guy if his alibi was confirmed by the FBI—unless it was a copycat killer.

Mitch paced back and forth, running his hand through his hair in frustration. All the Doms in the area were feeling it. One of their most important jobs in the lifestyle was to ensure their submissives were safe. At least ten dead women were proof no one was truly safe.

Disconnecting the call, Mitch threw the cell phone hard into the couch's cushions. "Fuck! Another sub is missing! Damn it!"

"Anyone we know?" God, Ty hoped not.

"Gina somebody. From Dark Desires up in Spring Hill." The public club was located about an hour north of Tampa, and this was the second submissive from there who'd gone missing. Their membership was far from adequately scrutinized, and any asshole could walk in off the street and start scening. It was one of the clubs Ty knew Mitch, Ian, and Dev hated even before the killings had started.

Mitch stalked into the kitchen and returned with two bottles of beer, a pizza box, napkins, and two plates. Within a few minutes they were both silently eating and drinking, but Ty was so tied up in knots, the sausage and pepperoni pizza tasted like cardboard, even though it was from his favorite pizzeria. He tried to make conversation. "So, what's the FBI doing about this guy?"

Wiping his mouth with a napkin, Mitch took a swig of beer before answering him. "What haven't they done? They've interviewed anybody and everybody, had a suspect profile done, and brought in one of the best serial killer investigators, who can be a bit of an arrogant ass. But apparently, his record of clearing cases is one of the best, so that's the man we want."

The conversation changed to another subject, and when Ty finished the pizza he didn't remember eating, he placed his beer and plate on the coffee table. Resting his forearms on his knees, he studied Mitch. Ty had gotten stuck at work the other night with an overseas conference call. He'd given Tori permission to have dinner with Mitch and play afterward. It was the first time it had just been the two of them, but Ty had been okay with it. He'd actually been glad to have someone to share the responsibility of taking care of Tori when he couldn't.

Tonight, she was on an overnight trip with one of the women who worked with her to pick up three new dogs she'd be training for a private security company in Jacksonville. It was a six-and-a-half-hour round trip, so they decided to break it up into two days.

Ty cleared his throat and tried to tamp down his anxiety. He was always waiting for the other shoe to drop around Mitch. "So, what did you want to talk about without Tori being here?"

Tossing his empty paper plate on top of the pizza box, Mitch leaned back in his recliner. "I've been thinking lately. What do you think about getting Tori a collar from both of us?"

His jaw dropped. That wasn't anywhere near what he'd expected to hear. "Um..."

"I know it's out of the blue, and we never discussed collaring before, but the other night, with her in the club, it felt odd having her on my arm with your collar around her neck and you nowhere to be seen."

Standing, Ty paced just as Mitch had done earlier. *Was he fucking serious? He wants to co-collar Tori? What about me, damn it?*

Stopping short, he glared at Mitch, anger roiling off him. His voice lowered to its Dom-tone almost on its own accord. "No. No fucking way. With all due respect, go to fucking hell, *Sir.*"

Mitch arched an eyebrow at both the denial and

the manner in which it was spoken. Getting to his feet, he crossed his arms over his chest and scowled at Ty. "On your knees, subbie."

Oh, shit. They hadn't been in D/s mode a moment ago, but Ty had inadvertently opened that door with the obnoxiously uttered title. He was torn between obeying the Dom, who sent shivers up his spine and got his dick hard, and standing his ground.

"Either say your safeword or get on your knees. I won't tell you again."

Despite his clenched jaw and fists, Ty slid to the floor. He spread his knees, bowed his head, and clasped his hands behind his back. "Yes, *Sir.*"

"Lose the pissed-off tone, Ty, or you'll face a punishment you won't like at all."

Taking a deep breath, he let it out slowly, trying to control his resentment. When he spoke again, his tone was much more submissive. "Sorry, Sir."

Mitch snorted. "Not yet, you're not. Now, explain to me what the problem is. Why don't you want me to co-collar Tori with you? Are you afraid of losing her?"

"No, Sir."

When he didn't continue, Mitch stepped closer. "Then what is it, Ty? Communication, remember?"

This time, it was Ty who snorted. "Practice what you preach, *Sir.*"

Without warning, Mitch grabbed the front of Ty's shirt and hauled him to his feet before shoving him against the wall. Two fury-filled gazes met. "What the fuck are you talking about?"

Ty fought the urge to swing at the Dom. That would be a surefire way for things to go to shit quickly. Instinctively, he knew Mitch wouldn't hurt him, so it was best not to instigate a brawl. Instead, he squeezed his fists tighter as Mitch held him in place. "You want to know? Fine, I'll fucking tell you. I'll never consent to co-collaring Tori until you decide where I stand in this relationship."

"What—"

His voice got louder with every statement that poured out of him. He could no longer hold it all in. "I'm tired of hiding in the closet, *Sir*! You want to fuck my ass? Fine, it's yours! But I want more, *Sir*! Either you stop holding back, or you walk away. I love you, damn it! Somewhere along the line, I fell in love with you as much as I love Tori, and I refuse to be your dirty little secret any longer!"

Mitch's eyes flared, and his grip on Ty's shirt tightened. Ty's heart sank—he'd fucked up big time, and there was no turning back. He opened his mouth to apologize, even knowing it was a waste of breath, but nothing came out as Mitch slammed his mouth down on his. *Holy hell!*

This was what he'd wanted. Had prayed for. Their tongues dueled and danced. The space between their bodies disappeared as Mitch pinned him against the wall and grabbed his hair with both hands. His scalp almost shrieked with pain, but that just drove his desire harder. His cock hardened and rubbed against Mitch's own erection through their jeans. The kiss was far from gentle, but Ty didn't care. He wanted everything the other man would give him and more.

Tearing his mouth from Ty's, Mitch gasped for air as he stepped back. The combination of anger, lust, and confusion normally on his face when they scened was missing. The only thing showing now was... love. But the three words Ty was dying to hear didn't flow from the Dom's mouth. "Strip, subbie. You have less than a minute to get naked and in my bed."

Holy fuck! "Yes, Sir."

Ty practically ran into the bedroom, kicking off his sneakers and throwing his clothes in all directions. He jumped onto the bed and lay flat on his back, his heart pounding. Moments later, Mitch entered the room, carrying his toy bag. "Four corners."

Without hesitation, Ty moved his outstretched arms and legs so they pointed to the corners of the bed. Mitch dropped the bag on the bed between the sub's feet and pulled out a set of wrist and ankle restraints. It didn't take long for him to attach and connect them to the straps already on the four posters of the California king-sized bed. This wasn't a piece of furniture you could buy at just any store—it had been custom-made for the Dom. Plenty of hooks and straps and a St. Andrew's cross, which could be raised and lowered as needed, were built into the wooden canopy.

Climbing onto the bed, Mitch straddled Ty's waist and stared down at him. He was still fully dressed, but that didn't stop Ty from admiring the man's physique once again. The black T-shirt hugged his torso, and his blue jeans were faded in all the right places.

"All right, subbie. Let's have a chat."

Ty swallowed hard as he took in the Dom's irritated expression. "Yes, Sir."

"Lost that snark, hmm? Good. Because you've already racked up a shitload of punishments. Before we go any further, let me clarify something—when we're in D/s mode, don't you dare raise your voice to me again, or I'll shove a ball gag in your mouth so fast it'll make your head spin. Understood?"

"Yes, Sir."

"Good. Now, if you want to discuss something with me, let's discuss it. Communication, remember? If something is bothering you, tell me—without yelling."

Ty finally realized why he was shackled. He was stuck here until he said his safeword or Mitch decided to release him. He'd always found it so easy to talk to Tori, but he was on top then. Right now, he was on the bottom and at his Dom's will. *Shit.*

Silence permeated the room as Mitch waited. He made himself more comfortable, and Ty knew they'd be here all night if he didn't start talking. Inhaling, he let it out slowly, mindful of the tone of voice he needed to use. "Okay, Sir. Yes, there are things I'd like to discuss."

"Good. Let's start with that 'dirty little secret' comment."

Fuck. "That's the way I feel. It's like we're sneaking around, and you'll never let me out of the closet I'm stuffed in, Sir."

Mitch closed his eyes a moment before opening them again. "I'm sorry if I made you feel that way. You're right—we have been sneaking around. That's all on me, and you shouldn't have to put up with it. But you figured out long ago that you wanted to be with both men and women. I've only had a month or so to come to terms with it." He paused. "I need to talk to my family before it comes out at the club. Will you give me a week to do that?"

What? He said he'd tell everyone about the three of us within a week? "Y-yes, Sir. If that's what you need."

"Thank you. Now that that's out of the way... let's move to the next thing." Mitch reached back with both hands and found Ty's erection. The switch's eyes fluttered shut in sheer ecstasy and joy. "Look at me, subbie. Let me learn how to touch you—there's still so much about you I haven't discovered yet."

Ty's hungry gaze met Mitch's. Strong hands caressed his cock, until he thought he'd come from just that. Mitch's grip tightened as he studied Ty's responses. A thumb brushed over his weeping slit, and

Ty gasped. One hand dropped to cup his sac and roll it gently. The sweet torture was killing him, but as much as he wanted to come, he didn't want all of it to end—at least not yet.

"Enjoy it now, subbie, because, for the rest of the week, this cock is off-limits to Tori and your hand as punishment for yelling at your Dom."

Shit! Wait, what? Your Dom? That was the first time Mitch had ever referred to himself as Ty's Dom. He'd said it when speaking to Tori but never the other man.

Ty almost cried out when Mitch let go of him and climbed off the bed, but his mouth watered when the Dom grabbed his T-shirt and pulled it over his head, dropping it to the floor. He stepped into the attached bath and returned a moment later with a red bath towel before moving to the foot of the bed and climbing back up. "I'm sure my first blowjob is going to be messy—lift your hips so I can put this under you."

Holy fucking shit! Still restrained, Ty awkwardly did as he was told, then relaxed on top of the towel. Mitch's hand closed around Ty's stiff cock again and pumped it a few times. His gaze followed the up-and-down motion as he licked his lips. Ty wanted to beg him to put those lips and tongue where he wanted them the most, but he didn't want to get in trouble for topping from the bottom again. Besides, this was all new to Mitch—he needed to go at his own pace.

The Dom's gaze met Ty's as he slowly lowered his

head. "Let me know if I do something you don't like." He grinned. "Or something you do like, so I can do it again."

Holy shit. Holy shit. Holy! Shit!

Mitch's mouth opened, and he took the purple tip of Ty's cock between his lips and licked the head. Ty saw stars. There was no way he was going to last long. *No way in fucking hell!* He tried to count backward from one hundred as Mitch's tongue rasped against his hard flesh. The taste probably wasn't odd for the man since he'd French kissed Tori after Ty had come in her mouth the other night.

Mitch's tongue curled around the girth, not missing a single inch, before sealing his lips and sucking hard. The sensations were driving Ty wild, and he moaned and tried to keep his hips from thrusting upward. *Don't top from the bottom. Don't top from the bottom. Stay still.*

A hand cupped his balls and gently rolled them as Mitch took him deep and swallowed. Ty gasped. "Fuck! That—that... do that again! Oh, God, please do that again! *Mmmm...* ssshhhit!"

Ty knew from experience that it didn't take long for a guy to learn how to give blowjobs, especially after being on the receiving end of them for so long. It was similar to a woman going down on another woman for the first time. Just do what you like to have done to yourself and all should be good. But that didn't mean the end of the act would be perfect. Almost every first-time blower ended up spitting instead of swallowing —it just took some getting used to.

Minutes or hours ticked by—Ty had no idea how much time had passed. He just knew he was in heaven. The only things that could improve it were if Tori was there with them and Ty was allowed to use his hands to guide the other man. Mitch's head bobbed up and down as he licked and sucked. Ty felt his balls tighten and a tingling in his lower spine, indicating he was close.

"Sir, if you don't want me to come in your mouth… I don't think I'm going to last much longer."

Mitch's tongue ran from the root of Ty's dick, up the underside, and along the thick vein. "Since this is the first time, I won't make you wait for permission. Come when you're ready."

Oh, thank God! The Dom's lips closed around the hard stalk again, and Ty felt a finger slide from his balls, across the tender skin, to his ass, and he lost it, screaming his release as Mitch sucked hard. As expected, the Dom coughed and spit when the stream of semen hit the back of his throat, but he replaced his mouth with his hand and pumped until Ty had nothing left to give.

Gasping for air and his head spinning, Ty stared at the man he'd fallen in love with. Mitch wiped his mouth with a corner of the towel, then sat back on his heels. "I was going to ask how I did, but that look of ecstasy tells me it was pretty good."

"Damn good, Sir. Damn fucking good."

Mitch reached over and undid both ankle restraints. "Glad to hear it." He stood and shucked off his jeans, revealing his own hard-on. "Now it's my turn."

Hell, yeah!

CHAPTER ELEVEN

Descending the grand staircase into the pit, Mitch nervously took in the crowd. In all his years in the lifestyle, this was the first time he would take center stage for a collaring ceremony. He'd collared several subs in the past, but they had all been contractual and temporary. This would be his first and last official ceremony if he had his way. He was off the market for good.

The other night, he sat down with his parents, brother, and sister-in-law and, after much babbling and hesitating, finally blurted out he was in love with a woman *and* a man. Thankfully, they were all open-minded, having a few gay marriages and relationships in the extended family. It also helped that when Mitch, Ian, and Dev had first started building The Covenant, they'd educated their families on the lifestyle they'd come to enjoy. While his folks, aunt and uncle, and brother never quite understood the draw, they supported and stood by the three club owners.

Thinking back to his mother's response to his announcement, Mitch smiled. After asking a bunch of questions about how the relationship worked, from both personal and legal standpoints, she'd been so happy he'd finally found love that she'd insisted he invite Tori and Ty for dinner last night. It had been an awkward first few minutes, but then Mitch's father, Dan, his brother, DJ—Dan, Jr.—and Ty had gotten involved in a conversation about business and stocks. Meanwhile, his mom, Janet, and sister-in-law, Meghan, had taken Tori under their wing. Before the evening was over, they'd received his family's blessing for the union.

Mitch had also sat down with his cousins and laid everything out. While Ian and Dev were as surprised as he'd been about his bisexual awakening, they'd congratulated him, then agreed to keep it to themselves until tonight's ceremony. After filling Tori in on everything that had happened the other day, Mitch and Ty asked if she was willing to amend her portion of their contract. The two men had already updated their relationship on it. When Tori had happily agreed, Mitch and Ty had gone shopping and picked out a permanent collar for her. What Ty didn't know was that Mitch had returned to the jewelers later in the day and selected a collar for him as well. He'd wanted it to be a surprise, and the platinum man's necklace was currently burning a hole in the front pocket of his leather pants. Instead of a collar, Ty thought he'd be going to get a BDSM symbol tattooed on his left shoulder blade in a few days with Mitch. They'd probably still do that, but Mitch knew Ty would love receiving the collar even more.

People congratulated Mitch on the upcoming ceremony as he walked among the members. But as far as they knew, it was just him and Ty collaring Tori together. After that, though, Mitch would order the switch to his knees and then profess his love to the man in front of the entire club.

God, he wanted to throw up. He hoped the anxiety he felt about being bisexual and being in love with a man would ease with time. At least, here in his club, among open-minded members of the lifestyle, he didn't have to worry about being judged. There was sure to come a time in public when they'd be ridiculed for their ménage relationship, but they'd deal with that when it happened.

While lying in bed a few nights ago, the three talked about moving in together. Mitch and Ty's condos weren't big enough for all of them. The little cottage Tori lived in now was also too small, so they planned to build a new house on the acreage of her ranch. Sometime next week, they'd meet with Parker

Christiansen, whose construction company had renovated the club, Trident Security's buildings, and Ian and Dev's penthouse-sized apartments on the far end of the compound, to look at plans.

Someday, down the road, they'd also talk about marriage and any children that may come along in the future. While it wouldn't be a conventional family, there were ways to make things legal, so if one died, the others were protected regarding finances and other matters. One of the two men would be legally married to Tori, while their lawyers would ensure all three were taken care of.

Mitch approached the central stage, where Ty stood talking to Ian and Devon. A large, leather-covered St. Andrew's cross sat in the middle of the elevated platform, which was only used for demonstrations and collaring ceremonies. Mitch's gaze roamed over Ty's bare chest, and he felt himself grow hard. Like Mitch, Ty wore black leather pants, a vest, and boots for the ritual.

When Ian saw his cousin, he held out his hand to shake and jutted his chin back toward the stairs. "Looks like we're ready to start."

Glancing back over his shoulder, Mitch's heart nearly stopped when he saw Tori standing at the top of the stairs. She was breathtaking in a sheer, white, lacy teddy covering her torso, with a matching thong and bare feet. Her hair was pulled into a romantic-looking updo, and her neck was devoid of the collar Ty had given her months earlier. The men had decided to redesign the simple leather and gold one for Tori to have for everyday wear, as the one they were presenting her with tonight was too elegant for her job.

Devon and Ian's submissive wives, Kristen and Angie, respectively, stood on either side of Tori, wearing black lingerie. They'd helped her get ready, and, similar to bridesmaids at a wedding, they would lead her to the stage. Tori had asked Master Parker to be her escort and present her to her Doms. The man was climbing the stairs to take his place next to her.

Turning back to Ty, Mitch smiled. "Ready?"

"Absolutely."

They followed Ian onto the stage. As head Dom of the club, Mitch's cousin would be the master of ceremony. Like weddings, collaring ceremonies varied in style, size, content, and location. Some people preferred to go small and simple, with only a few others in attendance, but Mitch had been at a few with full-blown receptions following the collaring. One of the first ceremonies held at the club years ago had been so beautiful and poignant, and many that'd followed had taken elements from it, and tonight would be no different. However, each ceremony had its own aspects chosen explicitly by the Doms and/or subs.

As Ty and Mitch attached small microphones to their vests, Ian picked up a hand-held one, and the music was turned off. "I think we're ready to begin. Submissives, please kneel."

Throughout the pit, men and women went down on their knees, where they would remain until the ceremony was over. Low chamber music floated through the club speakers as Tori began her descent. Standing side-by-side with Ty, Mitch watched as the woman they both loved walked toward them, her head bowed and eyes downcast. Angie and Kristen led the way, and Master Parker guided her to the stage. When they reached the bottom of the steps, both women moved to the side and knelt beside Devon.

Ty and Mitch stepped forward, each holding a hand out for Tori to take. When she let go of Parker's arm, her Doms led her up the stairs to the center of the stage, where she lowered herself to her knees on the large burgundy pillow that had been placed there.

The music faded as Ian spoke again. "Master Mitch and Master Tyler, do you wish to collar your submissive and vow to be her protectors?"

The men answered at the same time. "I do."

"Tori, are you willing to be collared by Master Mitch and Master Tyler?"

Her eyes still downcast, Tori answered, "Yes, I am, Sir."

"And are you doing so under your own free will?"

"Yes, I am, Sir."

"Extend your arms, sub."

As Tori followed the command, Ian handed Ty a long, white silk scarf. The switch took it and stepped forward. He wrapped the material around the sub's arms, starting at her wrists, binding them together to symbolize Ty's and Tori's union. When he was finished, Mitch wrapped an identical scarf around her arms on top of Ty's, ensuring it wasn't too tight.

After Mitch stepped back again, Tori lowered her bound arms, and Ian indicated for Ty to start his vows.

Taking the custom-made collar he and Mitch had chosen from his pocket, Ty stood in front of his submissive. "Tori, tonight I commit myself to you. I vow to love, honor, and cherish you. I will hold no other above you. You belong to me, and I vow to protect you from all evils for as long as I live on this Earth. Will you accept this collar as a symbol of my ownership and our devotion to each other?"

"Yes, I accept your collar as a sign of your owner-ship and our devotion. I will wear it proudly and vow to love, honor, and cherish you for as long as I live on this Earth, Sir."

Ty placed the diamond and platinum collar around Tori's neck and let the two open ends rest on her collarbones. He then moved to the side and let Mitch take his place. Filled with emotion, it took Mitch a few seconds before he began to recite the same vows Ty had said a moment earlier. When Tori repeated her words to him, he hooked the two ends of the necklace together with a platinum locket and closed it.

Ian placed the only two keys that would unlock the collar in Tori's hands, which were still bound at the wrists. "Sub, present your Doms with the keys to your heart and submission."

Tori handed one to Mitch and the other to Ty. "I now belong to you, my Masters."

As far as Ty knew, that was the end of the ceremony. He reached out to help Tori stand, but Mitch's hand on his arm stopped him. "Ty, remove your vest and kneel next to Tori."

Their submissive was the only person, besides Ian and Devon, who knew what was about to happen. She shifted over on the oblong pillow to give Ty some room, a broad smile on her face. But the switch just stared at Mitch in confusion. His brow was furrowed, and his jaw had dropped.

The Dom grinned. "Okay, let's try this again. Ty, if you wish to wear my collar, remove your vest and kneel next to Tori."

There were a bunch of delighted gasps and squeals from the audience, but Mitch ignored them all as Ty slowly shrugged out of his leather vest and handed it to Ian. He then turned his bare back on the crowd and lowered himself onto the pillow beside Tori. His stunned expression was almost comical, and Mitch bit his lip to keep from laughing.

Ian handed Mitch another long, white silk scarf as he spoke. "Master Mitch, do you wish to collar your submissive and vow to be his protector?"

"I do."

"Ty, are you willing to be collared by Master Mitch?"

Swallowing hard, Ty didn't take his eyes off Mitch even though his gaze was supposed to be directed at the floor in submission for the ceremony. It didn't bother the Dom, though, because he wanted Ty to see his love for him. "Yes, I am, Sir."

"Are you doing so under your own free will?"

"Yes, I am, Sir."

"Extend your arms."

When Ty held out his arms, Mitch wrapped the scarf around them, binding them together as he'd done with Tori. When he was finished, he pulled the platinum collar from his pocket. He'd chosen a different, more masculine design for Ty. It was a simple linked chain with a platinum and black onyx triskelion pendant. The three-part symbol was common among the BDSM lifestyle, yet didn't look out of the ordinary to the "vanilla" world.

Tears filled his eyes as he saw Ty's eyes water and spill over. "Ty, tonight I commit myself to you as your Dom. I vow to love, honor, and cherish you. I will hold no other above you. You belong to me, and I vow to protect you from all evils for as long as I live on this

Earth. Will you accept this collar as a symbol of my ownership and our devotion to each other?"

Ty's chin trembled, but his voice was loud and clear over the sound system. "Yes, I accept your collar as a sign of your ownership and our devotion. I will wear it proudly and vow to love, honor, and cherish you for as long as I live on this Earth, Sir."

As Mitch secured the collar around Ty's neck, a peace unlike anything he'd ever known came over him. After releasing their bound arms, he helped both subs to their feet. He drew Tori to him and then Ty until she was sandwiched between them. Lowering his head, he kissed her with all the love he felt. Tenderly ending the kiss, he looked at Ty over Tori's shoulder. Grabbing the man's head, he pulled him close and kissed him full on the mouth. Clapping, whistles, and shouts of "congratulations" filled the club.

Releasing Ty, Mitch straightened and smiled at him and Tori. These two people were the other parts of his heart and soul—pieces he hadn't known were missing before now—and he would never let them go.

If you're following the best reading order of the

Trident Security series and its spinoff series (which is available on my website), then up next is *Mountain of Evil: TS Omega Team Prequel*. Keep reading for a preview.

For the best reading order of the Trident Security series and its spinoffs, check out the printable list on my website - www.samanthacolebooks.-com/pages/best-reading-order.

Want to know what's coming next? Join my Facebook Group -
Samantha Cole's Sexy Six-Pack's Sirens...

Or sign up for my newsletter -
samanthacolebooks.com/mailing-list

Mountain of Evil
Trident Security Omega Team Prequel

C lick. Click. Click.

Resting her arms, Mallory Hart inspected the pictures of a bald eagle she'd just shot on her digital camera. Hiking in the San Juan Mountain range of the Rockies was one of the best places for her to shoot nature scenes, which she'd then upload to stock photo sites for sale. She currently had over a thousand of them on various websites, and the extra income helped pay for her college classes, textbooks, and supplies.

After taking a few more shots of the majestic bird soaring overhead, she glanced at her watch: 2:30 p.m.

She had about another hour before she had to start back down the marked trail. It was approximately two miles to where she'd parked her six-year-old, gray Toyota Corolla. Her friends thought she was crazy to go hiking alone on Wednesdays when she didn't have any classes scheduled, but she liked the solitude. It wasn't often she came across another hiker this far into the wilderness during the middle of the week, and she always made sure she didn't stray far from the main trail. Just in case she did run into trouble, in her backpack was the satellite phone her father, who was retired from the Marines, insisted she have since it was difficult to get a cell signal sometimes. There were also two bottles of water, a few granola bars, a compass, and spare batteries for her camera. Clipped to her jeans was a container of bear repellent.

A scurrying occurred behind her, and Mallory spun around to try and spot the small animal that had caused it. Her gaze flickered around the brush and trees, but there was no creature in sight. High above her, birds sang and squirrels chittered. The unusually warm weather in the mountains for late March had brought some of the wildlife out of hibernation early.

Squatting down, she tried to see if a red fox, wolverine, or porcupine might be looking for food. The sound had been too big to be a chipmunk or squirrel, and too small for anything larger. She searched high and low. *Nothing*.

A breeze lifted her blonde hair off her shoulders,

and an odd chill went down her spine, causing her to pull her lightweight jacket tighter around her body. She was in the middle of the wilderness, high on a dirt trail, surrounded by aspen, cottonwood, and evergreen trees, some shrubbery, and rocks, yet she felt as if she were being watched. There was a gentle, downward slope to the east, leading to the small lake, and a more precarious, upward one to the west.. Scanning the area around her, nothing seemed out of the ordinary. She hoped like hell it wasn't a cougar or wolf. A bear would make a lot more noise than those two carnivores—especially if it didn't realize Mallory was there.

Deciding to start back toward the parking area, she kept her eyes out for wildlife she could shoot with her camera and any that might be a threat. After glancing back over her shoulder a few times, she began to relax a little and her mind went to what her boyfriend had planned for their date tonight. She'd been seeing Kevin McCarthy for a few weeks now, and things were starting to get serious. He wanted to take things further, however Mallory was nervous about it. She wasn't a virgin, so that wasn't the problem, but she hadn't been lucky with men in that department. The boy she'd lost her virginity to at sixteen had been sweet while they'd dated, but he'd left her for a girl he met in college while Mallory was still a senior in high school. The only other guy she'd been with had been after high school graduation, and he'd dumped her shortly after she'd put out. She'd learned too late he'd only been looking for another notch in his bedpost.

Those were the only two men she'd ever slept with. Number three might have been a guy in her freshman year of college, but she found out the bastard in her English Literature class had a bet with his friends he would be in her bed in less than a week of dating. Mallory had sworn off the opposite sex for a while after that, concentrating on her schoolwork and photography instead. After a year of not dating, she'd finally broken down after Kevin had pursued her for several weeks. But with her past history of dating jerks, she was now gun-shy about sleeping with him.

She'd only gone about a quarter of a mile on the winding trail, when she stopped short. There was bear scat in the middle of the path, and from the stench, it was recent. It had to be, because she'd have noticed it when she came that way fifteen or twenty minutes ago.

"Shit," Mallory mumbled to herself. The unintended pun was lost on her as her gaze darted around again. "The last thing I need is a fresh-out-of-hibernation momma bear with her cubs."

Another rustling sounded to her left, and she shifted in that direction. Again, she couldn't help but feel like someone was studying her. She hadn't seen any hikers in over forty-five minutes, and the last ones had been two middle-aged women who'd been out birdwatching, and they'd been a lot closer to the parking area.

Letting her camera hang from the strap around her neck, Mallory unclipped the bear spray from her belt loop and carefully continued down the path. Rounding another curve, she gasped and froze when a large figure stepped out from behind a tree. Her heart pounded in her ears as she stared at the burly man dressed in military-style clothing. His unruly dark hair needed a trim and so did his beard and mustache. A jagged, two-inch scar ran from his upper lip across his right cheek. He was over six feet tall and almost as wide. A large knife was sheathed and strapped to his leg. While she didn't see any other weapons, that blade was enough to scare the crap out of her. Mallory gripped her bear spray tighter as the man grinned at her.

"Hey there, pretty girl. I didn't mean to scare you." His leer belied his rumbling words.

Mallory tried not to show she was afraid. Swallowing hard, she hoped her voice sounded strong and unaffected by the fear coursing through her. She pasted a fake smile on her face. "It's okay. You just startled me is all."

"Uh-huh." The man stepped forward, and Mallory moved backward. "I scared you. I can see it on your pretty face. What's your name?"

She knew better than to tell him the truth, so she

answered the first name that popped in her head. "Susan." *Sorry for borrowing your name, Mom.*

"Susan. Pretty name for a pretty girl."

The way he kept calling her "pretty" sent shivers down her spine. He took another step closer, and her gut churned. "Thanks, but if you don't mind, I'm in a hurry. I'm meeting people back at the parking area."

An ugly sneer crossed his face. "Oh, I don't think anyone is waiting for you. I think you're lying and I don't like when people lie to me."

When the creep moved even closer, she started to lift the bear spray, more than willing to press the red button if she had to. Suddenly two arms wrapped around her torso from behind, pinning her own arms to her side. She screamed as she was lifted off the ground, her body twisting, trying to get loose. The spray bottle dropped out of her hand as she flailed her arms and legs. The man in front of her laughed when she tried to kick him, and grabbed her ankles with his dirty paws, holding them to the side. Mallory opened her mouth to scream again, but her throat went dry and her eyes widened when he unsheathed the huge knife and held it in front of her face.

"Stay quiet, pretty girl, or I'll cut you into little pieces."

Sitting in the cockpit of Trident Security's jet, Ian Sawyer stared out at the blue horizon above the gray clouds below. Beside him, his pilot, Conrad "CC" Chapman, a retired Air Force captain, was thankfully not in a talkative mood. They were flying the Omega team to Colorado for their final training mission before letting them loose without being under the watchful eyes of the six members of the original Trident team. The plan was to drop them in the wilderness with the bare-bones minimum of supplies and a two day hike back to civilization to see if all the months of bonding and training had paid off. With new governmental and civilian contracts and missions coming in weekly, Ian and his brother, Devon, who co-owned the private security company, had spent the past sixteen months or so putting together another cracker-jack team. In addition to a West Coast team, which was still in its infancy as well, they would no longer need to subcontract additional personnel for many of their missions and cases. But all of that was not in the forefront of Ian's mind.

Back in Tampa, another submissive from the BDSM community had gone missing, and it was probably only a matter of days before her mutilated body would be found at some public spot. Brenda Arliss would be the serial killer's twelfth victim, unless she'd disappeared under other circumstances, which Ian doubted. He and Devon, along with their cousin Mitch, also co-owned an elite, private, BDSM club, and were worried one of The Covenant's subs would be targeted before the FBI and TPD figured out who the killer was. Hell, just knowing any woman, sub or not, from his club or not, had been tortured like the victims had been burned in his chest.

Six weeks ago, one of the Doms from The Covenant had been brought in by the FBI for questioning, but had been released due to insufficient evidence. A DNA test and the solid alibi of being under surveillance by the FBI when Gina Spinak, the eleventh victim, had been snatched, had assured his innocence. The Dom apparently also was able to account for his whereabouts for when several of the other women were abducted, but was being stubborn about revealing the information unless it was absolutely necessary. Ian figured it was because he'd been with a submissive who was in the public eye, but he couldn't be sure. Either way, the man was no longer a suspect, but that meant the FBI/Tampa PD/Trident Security task force was back to square one—again. Despite the head of the local FBI's objections, TS had been brought in as consultants due to their connections and involvement in the lifestyle.

The door to the cockpit swung open and Tempest "Babs" Van Buren stuck her head in. "Coffee? I'm making a new pot because Batman's is crap that's not fit for human consumption."

Babs, short for her call sign "Bad-ass bitch," had been an Air Force helicopter pilot who'd been assigned to assist Ian's SEAL Team Four and a Marine unit in Afghanistan years ago. Her moniker hadn't come from an attitude problem, but because she'd been one of the most talented and bravest helo pilots around. She'd received numerous commendations during her tours in the devil's sandbox, the last one being a Purple Heart after coming under heavy enemy fire while extracting a few Marines from enemy territory. The tail rotor of the helo had been hit and failed, but thanks to Babs's talent in the sky, they'd been able to get far enough away from the hot zone, before she had to do a hard landing. What the Marines who were with her hadn't known until after the crash was she'd taken two bullets in her left leg, shattering the tibia and fibula, yet she'd still managed to fly the disabled bird. The doctors might have been able to save her limb had it just been the initial injury, but further damage was done when they crash landed. After being rescued, she'd been flown straight to a military hospital in Germany, where all efforts were exhausted before they'd finally amputated the leg before sending her back to the States to recover.

Before the female captain had been released from the hospital here in the US, Ian had gone for a visit and offered her a job with Trident. Once she'd gotten over the shock that she was still going to be able to fly a helicopter for missions, she'd accepted. Now, when she wasn't piloting their MH-X Silent Hawk, a military-grade, stealth bird, she was also an ace mechanic and maintained their fleet of vehicles, along with new hire Russell Adams. Most people didn't even realize Babs used a prosthesis unless they saw it. After training with the Trident boys for the past few months, she was entering her first marathon since losing her leg, having completed several of them while still in the Air Force.

CC waved Babs off, but Ian stood, and when the woman stepped back into the cabin, he followed her to the rear of the jet where there was a fully stocked kitchen. The rich aroma of coffee, which couldn't be coming from any convenience store brand, hung in the air, tantalizing his nose and making his mouth water. He grinned. "What? You don't like sludge anymore? You used to suck that shit down in the sandbox."

She let out an unladylike snort. "That's because I had no choice. Here, I do." Opening a cabinet, she pulled out a bag of whole beans from the Death Wish Coffee Company, dubbed "the world's strongest coffee" and a grinder he hadn't known was in there. "I made sure to hide my own stash on board."

"Damn, woman, you're a saint." Grabbing a clean mug, he handed it to her to fill.

"Saint Babs." She smirked as she poured the coffee and handed it back to him. "I kinda like that. Although, I'm sure all the dead popes would roll over in their tombs if I was canonized."

Taking a sip of the dark brew, Ian's eyes fluttered shut as his taste buds rejoiced. "Fuck, that's good.

Hide it from the peons out there. They haven't earned it yet. Hell, they may never earn it. When we get back to Tampa, order a case of this and stash it in my office. It's almost better than sex." When Babs lifted an eyebrow at him, he shrugged. "I said almost."

"Uh-huh."

Shaking his head, Ian turned and studied his new team, who were scattered about the luxury jet's seating. They came from a variety of military branches and law enforcement agencies. Cain Foster was sleeping in one of the recliners. The former Secret Service agent was very experienced with flying all over the United States and could fall asleep on a plane before it'd even taxied down the runway. Ian had seen him doze through several flights only to wake up completely refreshed as soon as the landing gear was lowered. He'd been one of their first hires for Omega and had quickly risen to the top of their list of who would lead the team. In the end, they'd chosen him and Tristan "Duracell" McCabe, who was sitting on one of the couches reading a political thriller, to be co-leaders.

McCabe was a retired Army Ranger, who'd been shot in the arm a scant few weeks before his last tour in Afghanistan ended. He'd still been recovering from the wound when he'd come to work for Trident. Both men excelled at leadership, and had experience and knowledge the other didn't possess—Foster was skilled in personal protection and dealing with social settings, and McCabe was an ace when it came to desert and jungle warfare. Together, they'd been the perfect choice to lead the team.

Lindsey "Costello" Abbott and Logan "Cowboy" Reese were sitting at a table with a backgammon board open between them. Abbott was a retired Marine sniper with an impressive number of combat kills. Despite her experience in war, she was a laid-back person off duty. She was pretty hot, too, which she used to put her enemies at a disadvantage—she didn't look deadly, and by the time people realized she was, it was too late for them. She'd quickly earned the respect of both the Alpha and Omega teams during training exercises and a few missions and cases she'd been involved with so far. While Jake Donovan, the Alpha team's sniper, had been out in San Diego for the past year and a half putting together the Trident Security West Coast team, Lindsey had filled in on both Tampa-based teams.

When they'd been going through the candidates for Omega, Ian and Devon had known they were taking a huge chance on hiring Reese. The former MARSOC—Marine Corps Special Operations Command—Raider had been one of seven Marines taken hostage by insurgents in Iraq thirty months ago. Two of them, Reese and another man, had been the only ones to survive the week as ISIS prisoners of war. The others had been tortured to death, and the remaining two Marines had been scheduled for the same fate before being rescued by a joint MARSOC-

SEAL operation. Reese was still dealing with PTSD, but as far as Ian could tell, he had it under control with the help of weekly therapy sessions, which were mandatory for him to remain with Trident. Despite his traumatic experience, he'd already proven he was a kick-ass addition to the team.

Sacked out in another recliner was Valentino "Romeo" Mancini, the pretty-boy of the group. Like many people had said about Jake Donovan over the years, Mancini had "Hollywood" looks. That and his apparent "love 'em and leave 'em" attitude toward women and relationships had led to his moniker. The retired Army SF soldier had come to Trident from the FBI Hostage Rescue Team, bringing his own experience in dealing with certain critical scenarios.

Darius "Batman" Knight had been a known entity to Ian and Dev before joining Trident, having served on SEAL Team Four with the original six-man Alpha Team. After several tours, and dozens of dangerous missions, he'd heard Trident was looking to expand and had immediately put his name in the hat of potential candidates. It had been a no-brainer for him to be offered one of the positions.

Rounding out the team, the final member was Kip "Skipper" Morrison, a retired Army SF and Los Angeles Police Department sniper, who was watching a movie on the TV with Batman. He was originally from the Tampa area and had taken the position with Trident in order to come back and help his family. His parents were divorced, and his father had remarried and had two younger children. When their father and step-mother had been killed in a car accident, Kip and his sister had stepped up to raise their half-siblings, a boy and a girl, ages nine and thirteen, respectively. They were still catching flak from their mother, who'd remained bitter about her divorce after all these years, but Kara, an elementary school teacher, and Kip knew they were doing the right thing raising the orphans. Ian gave them a lot of credit. So far they were doing a fine job as the children's guardians.

After the months of training, Ian was convinced he and Devon had chosen well, and was confident there would be no regrets. Back in Tampa, the new team also had Nathan Cook as their support contact. The uber-geek had been hired from the NSA—National Security Agency, and Trident had needed to get permission from the government to bring the man into the private sector. Thankfully, the contract they'd all signed enabled Cook to still log into the NSA's mainframe for research, since most of Trident's missions were the result of government contracts.

Once they landed at a small airport outside Montrose, Colorado, they'd drive into the mountains to a small town named Ouray. Then tomorrow, the team would board a Blackhawk helicopter with Babs at the controls. It'd been easier to contract out a local, private aircraft instead of flying their own bird from Florida to Colorado. The flight company's pilot had agreed to ride shotgun as Ian had wanted his entire staff working as they would in the field. The team would fast rope into the mountains with a two-day hike out. Provisions would be minimal, ensuring they worked together for survival. They would have a satellite radio, which was only to be used in life-or-death situations—a broken leg wouldn't qualify. With their combined experience, they'd easily be able to get their injured party back to the extraction point.

Movement from the two rows of first-class-style seating at the front of the jet caught Ian's eye. A pair of arms stretched over the back of the seat, and he smiled. His wife/submissive Angie had woken from her nap. He took a step forward then stopped and glanced down at the coffee in his hand. Grimacing, he sighed, took a final mouthful of the delicious brew, and poured the rest down the sink.

Bab's stared at him, horrified. "That's a sacrilege."

"I agree, but the smell of coffee is one of the things that turns Angie green at the moment. Until her morning sickness passes, I can't bring it within ten feet of her."

Chuckling, she toasted him with her mug. "And you called me a saint."

He opened the galley's refrigerator and grabbed a bottle of Coke and another of ginger ale. Striding through the cabin, his stomach growled—if he was hungry, then Angie must be starving. He never thought there would come a day when she would out-eat him, but when she wasn't sick to her stomach, she was filling it, which was fine with him. What wasn't fine was that some of her food cravings made his own stomach sour. Pickles and ice cream had nothing on his wife's choices these days.

"Nice to see you awake, Angel." He held out the bottle of ginger ale to her. "Did you sleep well?"

Her face lit up when she saw him, and she patted the seat next to her, before taking the soda from him. He felt a stirring in his groin as he sat. Fifty years from now, when they were old and gray, she'd still be beautiful and make him want her. "Thank you, and yes, I did. Where are we?"

"About an hour from the airport. Do you want something to eat?"

Before she had a chance to answer, her stomach did it for her by rumbling. Ian smiled and placed his hand on the small swell of her abdomen. He couldn't wait to see her belly grow with their child because she really wasn't showing yet. But her breasts had already grown larger and more sensitive, which he loved.

"What's on the menu?"

"I had food services stock a few of your favorite, weird cravings."

Her smile grew, and he knew he was about to cringe at whatever she said next. "Bacon and Hershey's syrup?"

Yup, talk about a sacrilege. "No, but I can make you mayonnaise on cinnamon raisin bread, peanut butter and baloney on rye, or there's vanilla ice cream and honey barbecue chips." She loved to mix them together, and Ian couldn't stand to watch her eat it—or any of the other weird combinations of food, for that matter.

"A mayo sandwich, please. And a Yoo-hoo, if there is some."

Rolling his eyes, he stood. "I hope Jordyn craves that if Carter ever gets her pregnant." Their friend, who was a US spy, hated even looking at mayo for some reason.

Heading back to the galley, Ian knew no matter what his Angel wanted, he'd get it for her—even if it were something physically impossible, like the moon. However, that didn't mean he wasn't going to gag in the process.

Mountain of Evil is now available!

Dropped into the Rocky Mountains, the Omega team has minimal supplies and only two days to return to civilization...

Trident Security has grown by leaps and bounds, and to accommodate the increased caseload, they've compiled a team of seven—the best of the best from military and law enforcement backgrounds. But before they're turned out to handle their own assignments, the six men and one woman must first prove they're a cohesive and capable unit.

When the wilderness training mission becomes a real-life rescue op, will they all survive?

*This novella is a bridge between the original Trident Security (TS) series and the spinoff series, Trident Security Omega Team. While it is not necessary to read the original TS series or this prequel before the Omega Team series, it will give the reader more insight and background into the Alpha Team of Trident Security.

OTHER BOOKS BY SAMANTHA COLE

***Denotes titles/series that are only available on select digital sites. Paperbacks and audiobooks are available on most book sites.

THE TRIDENT SECURITY SERIES

Leather & Lace

His Angel

Waiting For Him

Not Negotiable

Topping The Alpha (MM)

Watching From the Shadows

Whiskey Tribute

Tickle His Fancy

No Way in Hell: A Steel Corp/Trident Security Crossover (co-authored with J.B. Havens)

Absolving His Sins

Option Number Three (MMF)

Salvaging His Soul

Trident Security Field Manual

Torn In Half

Burning For Him

*****Heels, Rhymes, & Nursery Crimes Series**
(with 13 other authors)
Jack Be Nimble: A Trident Security-Related Short Story

*****The Deimos Series**
Handling Haven: Special Forces: Operation Alpha
Cheating the Devil: Special Forces: Operation Alpha

The Trident Security Omega Team Series
Mountain of Evil
A Dead Man's Pulse
Forty Days & One Knight

The Doms of The Covenant Series
Double Down & Dirty (MFM)
Entertaining Distraction
Knot a Chance
Finding His Forever (MM)
Reclaiming His Soulmate

The Blackhawk Security Series
Tuff Enough
Blood Bound

Master Key Series

Master Key Resort

Master Cordell

Hazard Falls Series

Don't Fight It (MMF)

Don't Shoot the Messenger (MFM)

Don't Burn Bridges

The Malone Brothers Series

Her Secret

Her Sleuth

Her Savior

Largo Ridge Series

Cold Feet

*****Antelope Rock Series**
(co-authored with J.B. Havens)

Wannabe in Wyoming

Wistful in Wyoming (M/M)

Cock & Bull Series (M/M)

Scout

Rico

Standalones

Where the Broken Bloom

Scattered Moments in Time: A Collection of Short Stories & More

Sweet Revenge

The Sugarplum Fairy (M/M)

*****The Bid on Love Series**

(with 7 other authors!)
Going, Going, Gone: Book 2

*****The Collective: Season Two**

(with 7 other authors!)
Angst: Book 7 (M/M)

Special Collections
Trident Security Series: Volume I

Trident Security Series: Volume II

Trident Security Series: Volume III

Trident Security Series: Volume IV

Trident Security Series: Volume V

Trident Security Series: Volume VI

ABOUT SAMANTHA COLE

USA Today Bestselling Author Samantha Cole is a retired police officer and paramedic who now writes heart-pounding romance in multiple forms—MF, MM, and ménage. From military heroes to rugged cowboys and small-town heat, her stories blend passion, loyalty, and danger in perfect balance.

Awards:

Wannabe in Wyoming (co-authored by J.B. Havens) won the bronze medal in the 2021 Readers' Favorite Awards in the General Romance category.

Scattered Moments in Time won the gold medal in the 2020 Readers' Favorite Awards in the Fiction Anthology category.

Where the Broken Bloom (formerly *The Road to Solace*) won the silver medal in the 2017 Readers' Favorite Awards in the Contemporary Romance category.

Sexy Six-Pack's Sirens Group on Facebook
Website: www.samanthacolebooks.com
Newsletter: samanthacolebooks.com/mailing-list

facebook.com/SamanthaColeAuthor

instagram.com/samanthacoleauthor

bookbub.com/profile/samantha-a-cole

goodreads.com/SamanthaCole

amazon.com/Samantha-A-Cole/e/B00X53K3X8

tiktok.com/@samanthacoleauthor

youtube.com/@SamanthaACole-bp6yu

www.ingramcontent.com/pod-product-compliance
Lightning Source LLC
Chambersburg PA
CBHW061309210726

48293CB00003B/1177